ANGUS PETER CAMPBELL is a native of the Island of South Uist in the Outer Hebrides and was brought up there and on the Island of Seil in Argyll. His writing has won many awards over the years, including the premier Bardic Crown from the leading Gaelic organisation, An Comunn Gàidhealach. His Gaelic novel *An Oidhche Mus do Sheòl Sinn* was voted by the public into the Top Ten of the Best-Ever novels from Scotland. His poetry collection *The Greatest Gift* was reviewed as a masterpiece by Sorley MacLean, his poetry collection *Aibisidh* won the Scottish Poetry Book of the Year Award in 2012, and his novel *Memory and Straw* the Scottish Fiction Book of the Year Award in 2017. The writer, academic and singer Dr Anne Lorne Gillies has described him as 'an international literary figure alongside the likes of Gabriel Garcia Marquez, Toni Morrison and Laura Esquivel'.

GW00728913

By the same author:

The Greatest Gift, Fountain Publishing, 1992
Cairteal gu Meadhan-Latha, Acair Publishing, 1992
One Road, Fountain Publishing, 1994
Gealach an Abachaidh, Acair Publishing, 1998
Motair-baidhsagal agus Sgàthan, Acair Publishing, 2000
Lagan A' Bhàigh, Acair Publishing, 2002
An Siopsaidh agus an t-Aingeal, Acair Publishing, 2002
An Oidhche Mus Do Sheòl Sinn, Clàr Publishing, 2003
Là a' Dèanamh Sgèil Do Là, Clàr Publishing, 2004
Invisible Islands, Otago Publishing, 2006
An Taigh-Samhraidh, Clàr Publishing, 2007
Meas air Chrannaibh/ Fruit on Branches, Acair Publishing, 2007
Tilleadh Dhachaigh, Clàr Publishing, 2009
Suas gu Deas, Islands Book Trust, 2009
Archie and the North Wind, Luath Press, 2010
Aibisidh, Polygon, 2011
An t-Eilean: Taking a Line for a Walk, Islands Book Trust, 2012
Fuaran Ceann an t-Saoghail, Clàr Publishing, 2012
An Nighean air an Aiseag, Luath Press, 2013
Memory and Straw, Luath Press, 2017
Stèisean, Luath Press, 2018
Constabal Murdo, Luath Press, 2018
Tuathanas nan Creutairean, Luath Press, 2021
Constabal Murdo 2: Murdo ann am Marseille, Luath Press, 2022
Electricity, Luath Press, 2023

Eighth Moon Bridge

ANGUS PETER CAMPBELL

Luath Press Limited
EDINBURGH
www.luath.co.uk

First published 2024

ISBN: 978-1-80425-137-9

The paper used in this book is recyclable. It is made from
low-chlorine pulps produced in a low-energy, low-emission
manner from renewable forests.

Printed and bound by
Hobbs the Printers Ltd., Totton

Typeset in 10.5 point Sabon by
Main Point Books, Edinburgh

I

I'M NOT EVEN sure it was an island, though everyone called it The Island. Of course, before the bridge was built, it would have been, though there were some arguments over that too. Hadn't the ancient tribes placed shoogly stones in the water so they could go across at low tide, and hear the stones moving when strangers – enemies – came calling? And didn't the Romans build a stone path for their chariots, which the Vikings then destroyed because what need did they have for solid roads when the seas and the oceans and the lochs and rivers were their highways?

But the bridge is modern. Relatively new, anyway. Built by General Wade to garrison his troops in the old castle, but – more importantly – to open up the island to trade and commerce with the mainland. So the islanders would not be so insular and clannish and suspicious and bloody-minded, but would learn that the mainland merchants posed no danger to them. Dissolute mainlanders who had no strength because they didn't eat enough fish and wore thin, useless clothing. Who carried no swords or flames of fire. They just wanted to make a bit of money and sell shoes and horses and nails to the islanders. And the mainland wives and women and girls could be as charming and able to bear as many heavy loads of peats on their backs, and as many children, as the island women. It's a pretty, arched bridge. They say the rebel pirate Olghair MacKenzie hid his priceless Spanish treasure in it after the Armada, but only children and old people believed that story.

All that's history. For the bridge now carries an endless stream of traffic across, day and night. The early morning school bus, and the forestry van and the fish-farm lorry and all the individual cars taking hotel and office and road workers into the nearest large town, and the bread van and the fish van and the library van and the coal lorry coming over the other way bringing sliced bread and filleted haddock and books and trebles to the island, and – of course – all the visitors and tourists coming over the bridge for the day, just to see what The Island is like. Is it as pretty as it looks in the pictures?

It's bare and rocky on the north, towards the open sea. And green and lush on the south side, where the bridge and the firth and all the gardens are, smelling of lilac and wild garlic and buddleias. That's where we came to stay.

My father was the schoolmaster. We'd always lived in the city, but this job came up. I didn't know anything about it until the whole deal was done and Dad announced to me one night after supper that we'd be leaving and going north in a month's time. North. There would probably be snow and lots of ice and we might even live in an igloo and wear furs and sealskins to bed as in the books. Though it was never that far north. Just a hundred miles up the road.

'It's like Treasure Island,' he said to me. 'Loads of caves and coves and rocks and hills and hiding places.'

'And pirates?' I asked.

He laughed.

'Not unless you and I become one!'

I don't think Mum wanted to go. As I sat in my bedroom upstairs, reading, I could hear their voices. Dad calm and measured, in that quiet voice which I knew annoyed Mum so much. I heard her once saying,

'Why don't you speak normal? If you're angry, just speak in an angry voice rather than in that sweet puddingy way.'

I thought it was funny. But that was the voice he was now using, and though I couldn't hear what Mum was saying I knew by her higher pitch that she was annoyed. 'Shop,' I heard her say, and 'flowers', but then Dad's soft reasoned voice resumed again, then there was silence.

We arrived on The Island in early summer. Mum made all the arrangements, because she was the one who did that kind of work. I helped her a bit, putting books into boxes and cutlery and pictures and ornaments into crates and labelling them.

Especially labelling them, because I was good at writing and I liked using the non-smudge pens. Magazines, I wrote on one box. And Gardening Books on another. And Cooking. Knives. Forks. Spoons. Plates. Pots. Careful DO NOT SHAKE I wrote on the big box with Mum's three small Delftware vases, well wrapped between tea towels and protected by brown wrapping paper. And they survived, taking pride of place on the dresser in the living room of our new home.

I was ten and just finishing Primary Six. Dad said he would have preferred to have moved a year later, when I finished Primary Seven. That would have been a cleaner break for me, without having to change from one primary school to another. But really he had little choice, because the job advert was one of those once-in-a-lifetime opportunities he didn't want to miss. It was unlikely to happen again.

Term time finished on a Friday, so we moved the first weekend of the summer holidays. The removal men came in the morning while I was still at school and when I came back home at three o' clock everything was already inside the van. It was strange seeing the house empty, except for the things we couldn't take: the bath and fireplace and flooring and kitchen units. I could see all the scratches and marks and dust and drawings on the walls, no longer hidden by tables and chairs and dressers and cupboards.

My crayon drawing of a dinosaur with fifteen legs and bright orange scales decorated the wall where the mirror had been, and the pencil marks of me growing bigger every birthday stretched up the window frame. I stood by the marks and was already taller than I had been on my last birthday. I was a bit sad that I couldn't add to it. Though the new people would probably paint over it anyway. And I would make new marks at the new house and see how high they would go.

Mum and I got a lift up to The Island in the removal van. It was amazing being so high up in the front of the lorry. We only had a small car, and I always sat in the back looking out at the traffic or playing some kind of game to pass the time. Green car blue car was one of my favourites, and the other one was counting the numbers on the buses that passed and adding all the numbers up to see if I could reach a thousand before we arrived at our destination. I never did, unless we drove out into the country and met a 916 or a couple of 502s.

But high up in the removal lorry I could see everything. The cars down below were like toys, and as soon as we left the city I could see for miles and miles across the fields and over the lochs and up into the sky where jet clouds crossed and passed each other. I sat between the driver and Mum, so I could watch him control the gears and the big driving wheel and the row of lights. He showed me how they changed from white to blue to orange at the flick of a switch.

'Orange when it's foggy,' he said, 'and blue when it's frosty.'

The most fun I had was listening to the sound the lorry made as we drove up past Loch Lomond and over the hills. It had eight big wheels and every time they hit a hole or bump in the road it made us all bounce up and down. Same as the time Dad had taken me to the Fair and we sat together on the horse that went round and round the carousel. Dad sat behind me, holding my waist, and we shrieked and laughed every time the horse galloped up and down while the man who operated it turned the big green and yellow wheel.

'This lorry has six gears,' the driver said. 'And they're all animals!' We were stopped at lights.

'See,' he said. 'When the lights turn green I'll put it into first gear. And that's a bear! Hear – deep and growly.'

And as the lorry moved he pushed it into second gear.

'A tiger,' he said.

Then third.

'Sounds like a lion,' I said.

Fourth was a leopard and fifth a panther. We leapt along the road, rivers tumbling on one side and the hills getting higher and higher as we climbed up into the Highlands. Everything was connected to everything else and could become something new, I thought. Otherwise how could all those rivers turn into big lochs and the lorry into all those magic animals? You could invent anything.

Our new house was next to the school, 1889 carved on it above the main door. It had a long hallway and stairs with two bedrooms at the top, one mine and the other kept for visitors. Mum and Dad's bedroom was downstairs at the back overlooking the garden. We had two big sitting rooms downstairs at the front, one where we all sat together to watch television and the other a 'best room' which we only used at Christmas or if some kind of special person like the minister or the school inspector came visiting. Then Dad lit the open fire and brought in the pine logs he kept in the shed to create the smell of Christmas for our guests.

I didn't do much of the moving in. Just carried some of my clothes and books and my train set upstairs to my bedroom, and that was more or less it. The removal men did the rest, with Mum supervising and Dad shifting bits of furniture from here to there. He would position a chair in the corner, then stand looking at it for a moment, humming and hawing, then move it a few inches this way or that. Same with all the pictures. Mum dealt with the bedrooms and the kitchen, putting everything in order.

Once we settled into the house, Dad started to get up very early most Saturday mornings and head off with his rucksack, and sometimes his tent, to go walking for the day. To get away from the stress of being surrounded by noisy children all week, he said. He'd come back late in the evening but sometimes did it the other way round, heading off after school on Friday and returning back home Saturday morning. Teaching was just a public obligation compared to this private joy.

'Can I come, Dad?' I asked, but he always said No.

'No, son. Not now. It's the only time I get space to myself. To do a few things on my own. You'll understand when you're older, Jack.'

I sat upstairs in the window seat looking at the sea. Our previous house looked out onto the Botanic Gardens and its large glasshouse full of plants from Mexico and China, and it was ever so hot, so on cold winter days Mum sometimes took me down there and I enjoyed floating a little wooden boat along the narrow stream that ran between the huge trees inside. I saw no boats at sea off The Island. Just some seagulls perched on the stone wall that protected the road from the tide.

I went outside into the new garden. An old glasshouse seemed to lean against the wall separating us from the school. There was nothing in it but empty shelves and baskets and buckets and plastic pots and a spade. We had an area of lawn and a big old pine tree that became my play area for years. It had a rounded hollow back which made a perfect cave and a low branch I could sit and swing on, and when I climbed further up a space I turned into my special den. It was like being high up in the cab of the removal van, because I could see everything from there: out west as far as the sea stretched and down the way towards the village where other children played in the playpark next to the hall. That first summer was long and hot. I was on my own, happy breathing the warm smells of the garden from the tree.

When I played in that tree it became more than the glowing globe in my Dad's study. The lower branches were the Nile and the Amazon and the Yangste and the upper ones Mars and Pluto and Jupiter, from where I could look down and see the small world far below twinkling in the dark.

I sometimes think that it was lying in the tree smelling pine needles that made me interested in chemistry. Though I had earlier moments. The Christmas logs in the open fire, and the buddleia in my granny's garden, the jasmine and lilac bushes that grew against the schoolhouse wall in the late evening sun. Their fragrance filled the air, and I fell asleep every night cradled by it.

We were fortunate. The school and schoolhouse were on the west side of the island, where the Gulf Stream keeps things warm. Even in winter, the wind and rain and frost and snow are soft and temporary, while over in the east, only three miles away, the wind was stronger, the rain heavier, the frost colder and the snow deeper. I missed some of that, of course, but always headed east with my sledge when the snow came to hurl down the big hill for hours on end.

I came to know that tree so well. Every knot and twist and turn and where I could lean and which branches were brittle and best avoided, and where it was best to sit in the summer (right at the bottom) when all the leaves were in bloom, or in winter (right at the top) when everything was bare so I could see across the village and beyond the immediate sea towards the distant islands which sometimes shimmered in the haze and frost.

Mum continued to make our new home our own, while Dad spent a lot of time next door in the empty school preparing it, and himself, for the new school year, which started late in August with the bell clanging just over the wall. He rang it the first morning, and then gave every pupil a turn at ringing it day after day all through the year. It was an old open bell and the harder you shook it the louder it sounded.

2

IT WAS A composite class. Primaries Six and Seven together, taught by my father. There were two other teachers – Miss MacLean, who taught the infant classes, as we called them, One, Two, and Three, and Mrs MacInnes who taught the middle classes, Four and Five.

Of course everyone knew I was the headmaster's son and treated me with caution. I would probably tell on them. Tell-tale tit. When I got back home and had tea, what else would The Headie's son speak about except what Johnny had done behind the bike shed and the language Maggie used on the playground? As if either of us had any interest in finding out. I ate fast and left the table as soon as was decent, and Mum and Dad were too worried about other things to concern themselves with what the village children said or did.

I hated Dad being my teacher. My previous school had individual classes. He taught Primary Seven while I had Miss Sinclair. She was tall and thin and had a slight lisp and always finished our work for us so that we all got good marks. The annoying thing about Dad as a teacher was that he behaved publicly in front of the class as he did at home. Those embarrassing little habits which I'd have preferred to stay private. The way he stuck his pinkie into his ear when he was searching for the right word and the way he scratched himself when one of the children annoyed him.

My best friend that year in primary school was another incomer to the island, Sally Henderson. Her father had died in an accident and her mother had returned back home after years away. I suppose we both felt that we were outsiders, intruders. It's not that anyone was unfriendly or anything, just they'd all grown up together and knew each other, and each other's families, in a way that Sally and I never could. John was Bob's brother, and their cousins were Linda and Cathie and Mary. They all shared bikes and stories and comics. We were always included in their games but it felt like we were guests, for they were always explaining stuff to us as if we didn't know how to play hopscotch or the rules of walking backwards on the high wall. We tried to introduce games too. They never liked our ideas.

It's not that Sally and I played or talked together much at first. More like when we played collectively we were always put in the same team by whoever was leader and were only ever asked to lead if it was to their advantage. When we all played rounders, for example, they would always give the bat first to Sally because they had the best bowler in their team and wanted to get off to a good start. So Sally and I became a sort of team and the highlight of our Primary Seven year was when we won the three-legged race, hopping over the playground line well ahead of everyone else. We got a balloon each for a prize. Thankfully, it was presented to us by the school cook, Mrs Campbell, and not by Dad. It helped that Sally was a wonderful athlete, later representing the high school at the Junior European Schools Cross-Country Championships. She always smelt nice.

'Mint,' she said. 'It grows everywhere in our garden. So it does.'

She often said 'so it does' after saying something.

'To make sure it's true,' she told me.

I turned out to be a very good football player. I'd always played football, at first on the street outside our house in Glasgow with my wee pals Hughie, Sparky, and Sid. We called him Sid after the balloon-juggling dog in the comics, though his real name was James. He was a good goalkeeper and could catch any ball no matter how high or low or hard it was kicked or thrown at him.

We didn't play that much football at the new school, though. Officially anyway. Partly because there weren't that many of us, and partly because most of them preferred to do other things. We had no school team as such and when we played it was a kickabout in the playground or, when it was dry, on the long strip of grass outside the school wall. Because I wanted to be better pals with them, I pretended to be a mediocre player (though they might have been more impressed had I shown off my skills) and always said I would play in goals rather that outfield, where I could have dribbled through and past them all and scored any number of goals. It's always good to be part of a team, making believe that there is a common cause.

But that didn't stop me practising and playing endlessly before and after school and at the weekends. Keepy-ups, headers, trapping, swirling, back-heeling, moving the ball from heel to ankle to knee to hip to shoulder to head and whack, there it was in the back of the net, which was a chalked circle at the very top of the school wall. I practised free kicks from over the wall, bending the ball at an arc into the small circle. And an endless number of penalties, sometimes with my right, sometimes with my left, and sometimes playing blindfolded, running around and between small chuckie stones which Sally placed for me in different positions to dribble round as she guided me between with shouts, 'Left! Right! Forward! Back!', so that my sense of positioning and moving between hazards became instinctive.

Sally herself was a good player too, though she didn't believe in it.

'I like the game,' she said, 'but don't see the point of all that scoring.'

'But that's the whole point,' I said.

The other children preferred to play shinty and rounders. And basketball, because one of the parents had, once upon a time, hung a fishing net shaped like a basketball net from the end wall of the school. We joined a long tradition of trying to score 100 in a game. They said that was the record set by Hamish MacLachlan years and years ago and no one had ever beaten it, though everyone tried and tried. Sometimes after school I practiced throwing on my own and once reached ninety-five, though that didn't count for anything because anyone could do that standing there on their own. It was quite another thing to reach a hundred during an actual game while all the other players were tackling you and getting in your way and blocking you and making sure you never got a clean throw.

Sally and I spent long times on the shore. She tended to gather things – little round stones and shards of coloured glass and various sorts of shells, while I mooched about and if I found an interesting kind of stone would shout across 'Waw! Look at that!' and she'd run over and inspect it this way and that and depending on whether it was good enough took it with her over to her own pile or handed it back to me. So then I'd wander about looking for the best kind of chuckie stone to skim across the water, and the best was always if I found a thin bit of slate. Sally was the better thrower, however. Her chuckie stones always skimmed longer and lighter than mine, no matter how hard I tried. She said it was because I tried too hard.

'Just relax,' she said. One day she put her hand round my wrist and caressed it for a moment and it went all loose. When I flung the stone it skimmed across the water as light as a feather, skipping longer than any other stone I had ever thrown.

Other days we'd cycle along to the shoreline gardens. Mrs Nicolson had the best one. It had a hedge maze that went round in circles and if you put something into the charity box she kept at the gate you could go in there and spend hours getting lost and found. Of course, after a while we got to know the maze so well we could do it with our eyes shut, but then we worked out variations, blindfolding ourselves and being led into the centre to see how long it would take us to find our way out walking backwards.

The hedge was a mixture of hazel and pussy willow and hawthorn and blackthorn with sprigs of wild roses here and there. I learned to feel and smell the differences between them all, so that even when Sally tied a scarf over my eyes I could smell that I was at the blackthorn section which turned towards the hawthorn and took you through the dog rose area into the open air. I always knew where she was by the aroma of mint.

A corner of the garden always caught the sun, and Sally and I often sat there to pass the time. Sometimes it was marbles, which I carried in my pocket. Rolling them across the grass to see which ones landed nearest the daisy line. Or placing three marbles in a row several yards away and then rolling the fourth marble to see which one of us could hit the one in the middle. That usually took ages, because the ground was uneven, and it was pure luck if Sally or I managed to score.

We sometimes held hands, but only to play games. Say if we decided on a skipping game, where I would hop on my left foot, and Sally on her right, to see how far we'd get before falling. Or if we played tig or climbing, and Sally would go up to the first branch of the tree and lean her hand down and help me up, and then I'd do the same for the next branch.

Though the best was when we lay side by side under the lilac tree or by the buddleia bush and gazed up into the sky counting the clouds or the passing planes or birds.

'A seagull.'

'Pigeon.'

'Skylark.'

'Bee.'

And we'd hold hands, sometimes twining our fingers together, and always the smell of buddleia and lilac all around us. The first love that is like the first day.

3

EVERYTHING CHANGED AGAIN when I went to high school the year after we moved. That was over on the mainland. We all travelled there by bus, with the usual pecking order all through the six years. The first years in the front seats and then in ascending order all the way up to the back seats where the sixth-year pupils all sat, ruling the roost. Although Sally and I were in the same year we never sat together on the bus, for all the teenage boys said that was a sissy thing to do. Everyone's ambition was to survive long enough to make it to the middle seat at the back during that final year when you could orchestrate all the seating arrangements and the stories that were told and the songs that were sung. I never made it that far.

The high school had a fantastic PE Department, run by Mr Girvan, a retired army sergeant major. 'Snap to it, lad,' he always shouted, so of course his nickname was Snappy. All the teams – the football and swimming and hockey and rugby and shinty and cross-country teams – were hugely successful because Snappy made sure everyone trained and worked collectively as a team. We had three football squads. I was in the First XI, and

Snappy made sure we were entered into every district and school competition.

'You're here to win, not to play,' he'd say before every match. 'By fair means or foul.'

And mostly it was the latter, thanks to Biff MacGregor, our brute of a centre-half who made sure nothing much ever passed him. I played up front, scoring an endless number of goals. I always saw Sally on the sidelines cheering me on.

We had streamed classes at high school and my favourite subject was chemistry. Not that it was called that at first – just science in the first two years, then it split into three: chemistry, physics, and biology. I chose chemistry, partially because the class was held in a glassy portacabin out the back of the school, and you could stand at one of the lab desks at the window and look across the fields to the high hills beyond which were always covered in snow in the winter. All the other classrooms in the school were closed in with only old Victorian windows high up filtering glimmers of light into the bleak rooms. I can still see the long blue flames from the Bunsen burners flickering on the walls as the snow fell outside.

We were taught by Miss Jameson, whose mother and father ran the chemist shop in the town. She had long slim fingers, a bit like the glass tubes we used for measuring and mixing various solutions. She wore nail polish that sometimes matched the colours of the chemicals in our test tubes. Amazing experiments which proved one thing could so easily become another. Like when you add glucose to methylene blue in a jar and shake it, and the blue becomes colourless. Then you stop shaking it and leave it, and it turns blue again. I wasn't too interested in the magic of it, but in how the magic happened.

It's all got to do with precision and measurements and the way one thing – every living thing – reacts and responds to everything else. Like when Dad stuck that pinkie in his ear in front of the class and my body would shiver with embarrassment. Everyone would think that I also did that, and maybe even worse. Or the way I sensed my skin prickling when Geordie Smith, the school bully, came near. Or – much better – when I'd see Sally in the distance.

Mind you, Geordie Smith became my protector as we progressed through high school, because he was such a keen football player. A big brutal brawny centre-half who admired the way I played up front, making sure his team won all the time. It was sad in a way, because I think what he respected were not the countless goals I scored to win games, but the way I scored them. The way I played. I could sometimes catch a glimpse of awe in the way he applauded my moves and passes and goals, as if he wished he could do that too. I suppose we all admire (or hate) what we can't do ourselves.

Some folk call it art, though it's not that at all. It's much more like chemistry. Exact and precise. Which, of course, is an art as well. An awareness that everything is connected, and that a marginal change here can make an enormous change there. Instead of passing the ball sideways, you pass it forwards, and suddenly turn defence into attack. Or how a centre-forward (nowadays called a striker!) can move a fraction backwards, moving the defender along, and then suddenly heel forward while he's left in his previous position. Same as the glucose in the methylene blue.

The best classes were the ones where Sally sat near me. We shared a desk in geography, which was the best time of the whole week. I noticed everything she did. The way she always flicked that wisp of hair behind her left ear, and how her left knee always crossed her right (and never the other way round). I could hardly breathe. Maybe we'd leave school together and run away and live in a lilac and buddleia covered cottage in Greece where we could run along the long white seawall and then throw skifflers into the Aegean all evening long while the sun set.

I was in fifth year when I was provisionally signed by Chelsea. We were playing the final of the Scottish Schools Cup in Stirling. One of the Chelsea coaches happened to be holidaying in the area and watched the game. I scored a hat trick in the first half, and after the match Snappy Girvan, who was also our bus driver, told me that a Mr Chapman wanted a word with me. Mr Chapman gave me his card with the CFC hallmark and said he was in the area for the week, and if my parents got in touch with him, he'd like to ask me down to London for a trial. It was what we all dreamed of.

Mum was worried, and Dad was delighted. He accompanied me down the following week. We travelled by train, and a cab picked us up at the station and took us out to digs near Harlington where we stayed for a week. Mrs Potter had looked after several young players over the decades, so she knew when to feed us and when to encourage us and when to warn us. I called her 'Gran' and stayed with her for the three years I was at Chelsea. You find support wherever you can.

I was signed as an Apprentice Player on the Friday. Dad said I needed to stay on at school until the end of summer term to finish my Highers, and they were happy with that. So was I. I got Five As: Chemistry, Physics, Geography, Maths, and English.

Two other boys boarded with Mrs Potter that first season. A lad from Wales, who dropped out after a couple of months, and Tony Curran, who remained a life-long friend. Tony played three games for the first team before a bad knee injury forced him to retire, after which he got involved in horse-racing and became one of the best racehorse trainers in Ireland. I go over to the Irish Derby at the Curragh every year to see him and reminisce about how young and foolish and innocent we all were. Thinking we were a team when, really, only fate and circumstances, not any plan or vision, had thrown us all together. We were just boys.

I played fifteen games for Chelsea. For the first team, I mean. Though it has to be remembered that those were the days when we were in League Division One playing teams like Charlton, Oldham, and Hereford! Long before the big money Abramovich era and all the millionaire players. I was on £45 per week. More than enough for the little I spent. We trained every day, except on match days and Sundays.

Tony was from Northern Ireland, so that helped, because most of the other players inevitably called me Jock, with all the usual baggage that went with it. I tried to correct them, saying my name was Jack, but like everything else, once a thing is said that's it. It all sort of worked, though never as it could – or maybe even should? – have. But what does? We had to balance so many factors. The training and coaching regimes were too haphazard and changeable – one week it would be weights and body strengthening, then long distance and endurance training, then sprints, so our bodies never got into any proper, regular rhythm. And the coaching was equally varied, depending on who was taking it. Coach A concentrating on ball skills, Coach B tackles, Coach C passing, Coach D dead-balls, Coach E running, and when it came to an actual game all we could hear in our heads were all these contradictory voices, one telling us to run, another to tackle, another to shoot, move, stand, swerve, and so on. The worst was when they'd stand there moving magnets on a board as if we could do the same thing: shift right, left, sideways, diagonally, in all kinds of perfect lines and angles. We all sat there, nodding our heads in agreement, knowing how foolish it was to pretend that anything would work out as planned.

I realise it sounds easy to advise myself to ignore all these voices, except that would have left me mute and isolated. What if I'm supposed to shoot at this point, and

I only pass? Or what if I was meant to tackle there, and I stood off? It was always better to play safe. To check who was on the sidelines and remember his particular instructions and do them to the best of your ability. You could never please them anyway, even when we won. We should have scored more. We shouldn't have conceded that late goal. We had to stop compromising our goal difference and league position and costing the club money. Any time they praised us for scoring a goal or winning a match or trophy, the manager always rubbed his hands in circles the same way Snappy did, knowing that success led to more success. I started to suspect what was really important. It was never about joy, only reward.

'Have you got a dog's nose or something?' Tony asked me one day. 'The way you sense things.'

And maybe I did. Or do. Thing is, I'm only good at nice smells. Sweet isn't quite the word, for that's just a bland, sickly fragrance – the sort of smell you inhale in a hairdressing salon or cosmetics shop. Despite all the efforts to recreate the natural, our noses tell us immediately when a thing is artificial. Maybe nature itself is the culprit, for how can it ever be replicated? How can you compare Chanel No. 5 to the smell of newly mown hay or the sea after a storm or lilac or buddleia coming into full bloom, or even the fragrance of the hops in the Edinburgh air on a foggy winter's day?

But Tony was referring to the smells which my teammates had become so accustomed to that they no longer noticed them. Sweat and wet socks and shorts and shirts and boots lying all over the place and the everlasting stench of Ralgex in the changing rooms. I can still sniff it from a thousand miles away.

One morning I had a call from Mr Chapman. I hadn't seen or heard from him since I'd signed forms.

'Jack. Jack,' he said. 'I hear good things about you. Good things. Good things.'

Nothing was said unless it was said twice.

'You're off tomorrow. Tomorrow, what about meeting up for a drink? A drink.'

We met at the Welfare Arms. Another man was with him.

'Peter,' he said. 'Pete Watkins.'

He was a goalkeeper. Played for the Saints. Just about the best keeper in the league. I didn't really drink, but I agreed to a half-pint.

'So, Jack,' Mr Chapman said. 'So, Jack. How's it going? How's it going?'

'Fine. Fine.'

It was catching.

'Digs okay?'

'Aye. Perfect.'

Another sip.

'Digs okay, and enough money?'

'Aye.'

'Things are dear, Jack. Dear.'

'I manage.'

'Yes. But. Yes, but. Thing is, Jack, there are always things. Things we need. Things we want. A nice house of our own, instead of a lodging room. A car. Holidays abroad. Overseas. Rewards. And there are ways to get them. There are ways. There are ways.'

He paused.

'The match is next Saturday. Saturday. The cup game.'

Ah, I said to myself. Ah.

'Thing is, about the cup game, Jack. Thing is. There's money to be made. To be made. Depending.'

'Depending?'

'Depending who wins. Say if it was a draw. And it went to penalties. Penalties!'

'Which I always take?'

'And which Peter here never saves. Never.'

'Except on this occasion?'

'Except on this occasion.'

'You mean I'd miss?'

'It's always possible. It's always possible to miss a penalty. Isn't it Jack? We all make mistakes.'

'And if I did?'

'Well, if you did, Jack. If you did, then...'

'I can't. Won't.'

He put his hand in his pocket and took out an envelope.

'Can't or won't?'

'Won't.'

He counted out the fifty-pound notes.

'Won't?'

'Can't and won't.'

And I didn't. Though sometimes I regret it. 'Ambition,

Jack. That's the problem. Always the problem, Jack. You lack ambition. It will be the undoing of you, lad.'

I missed the penalty anyway. I've often thought about it. I usually placed the kick into one of the top corners, but for some reason that day I changed my mind at the last minute and tried to hit it low, just inside the post. It went wide, and Chapman must have smiled to himself, having won the bet and kept all the money. You never really know what you believe until you do it.

And I think of Peter. As he stood there between the posts, hoping I'd miss. O, I'd studied him all right, and if the penalty kick taker looked to the right before kicking the ball Peter always dived to his left, and if he looked to the left then Peter dived to the right. I looked to the right and he dived to the left and the ball slid past the right-hand post and we looked at each other and smiled. Me because these things sometimes happen, and him because he thought I'd agreed to help him. Which I hadn't. Though he'd never know.

But I do. And it's stayed with me, that missed penalty. Because it was true, and not false. I hadn't cheated. One of those things that hadn't been bought or sold or planned or intended. Like the chemistry experiments that go right because they've gone wrong, or wrong because they've gone right, by accident rather than design. And you discover that the race is not always to the swift, nor the battle to the strong. You can't fix everything. I felt like you feel when the school exam question you've prepared for so well comes up and all of a sudden you don't know the answer.

Sally and I used to skateboard along the pier wall. It ran from the end of the school playground all along the shore down by the pier houses then round the other side to the quarry at the bottom of the hill. Only one person could go on it at a time, so the one who waited timed the other to see how long they'd take. Except. Except in a section round the back of the pier houses the person doing the timing couldn't see the skateboarder, and if the tide was out the one on the skateboard could take a shortcut through the stone arch, though that was cheating.

And it was ever so tempting to cheat, especially if Sally's time was better than mine, for she wouldn't know anyway, because it was such fine margins and the five seconds or so I'd gain through the shortcut was always possible anyway by going that bit faster, though it was ever so risky, at the quarry end. She wouldn't know if I ever cheated or not. But it was like the penalty. I would. And that makes all the difference.

It gnaws away at you. The knowledge you have something you shouldn't have, because you cheated. Took it from someone who might have longed for it. Needed it. Might have made all the difference in the world if they'd won that day. Or hadn't lost. And all those reasons you construct. The excuses, which can justify anything. Who knows? No one will notice anyway. It doesn't matter much. Or not that much, anyway. Except it spoils the silence, like a blue bottle on a hot summer's day.

4

I SUPPOSE I made it. And didn't. Not every player can say they played professionally. At Wembley. In the FA Cup. Where I missed that penalty! Yet it didn't last, except in the sense that everything lasts. When I hear whistles I look up. Is it kick-off time again, or a penalty? Passing parks, the calls and shouts and cries of children playing make me reach for my kit bag.

Kevin was the only one who lasted in the game. Played through until his mid-thirties and then became a coach and manager. I still see him there on the sidelines in his tracksuit on TV. Most of the others I've lost track of, except for a few I bump into now and again or keep in touch with on Facebook. Liam who set up a concrete-mixing company and made a fortune, and Gerry who retrained as a ship's engineer and worked on the cross-channel ferries for a while before settling down on the Isle of Man. I'm tempted to say one in a thousand, or in a million, made it through to being full-time professionals. Most of us are failures.

After I left the club, I stayed on in London. I moved out of Mrs Potter's and found myself a small flat by the Thames. In those far off days when a young lad like me could afford a river view. And I spent a lot of time either looking at it from the window or walking by it or sailing it on a barge. And I suppose, because I've never forgotten that first day we crossed the bridge, high up in the removal van, ever so slowly, while the driver was anxious that the bottom of the lorry would get stuck on the highest point, and he shouted 'Whoopee' when we started descending on the other side, whenever I went out for a run, I tried to cross as many bridges as I could. There are thirty-five, and you'd need to be a marathon runner to do them all in one go. My usual run was along to Battersea Park, crossing the Albert Bridge, and then returning on the north side. It took me an hour or so, depending.

But it's best to walk them. Then they're bridges, not just things to rush over, trying not to bump into people. And how beautiful they are. The curves and the arches and the wood and iron and steel. The work that went into them. All those engineers and bricklayers and stonemasons and joiners, with their saws and hammers and measuring instruments tucked into their dungarees as they sat on the half-finished walls or parapets having their tea break.

My favourite is probably the Richmond Bridge, simply because the old stone arches remind me of Clachan Bridge on the Isle of Seil. The so-called Bridge over the Atlantic. Mum and Dad and I used to spend our summer holidays there, walking and fishing. We always played a pitch-and-putt course, and Dad always won.

I got a job as a railway clerk with British Rail at Paddington Station. Selling tickets from behind a glass booth. It was a job for life if I wanted. Old Bob Redman was retiring after fifty years' service. He smiled graciously when he received his gold watch. And he made the joke they all made when given the watch: 'If you'd given me this fifty years ago, all the trains would have been on time!'

For me the job was something to keep me going while I decided what to do next. And it was fine. Shift work, the best being the early morning one from six o'clock, finished at two and leaving me the rest of the day to do whatever I pleased. I started playing football again. I'd almost forgotten what it was like to play purely for the fun of it. Sunday League football, when it didn't matter much if you missed a tackle or misplaced a pass or scored a penalty or not. I know the team would moan and swear at each other, but none of the mistakes really mattered.

'That's a fortune you've cost us today,' the Chelsea manager had said to me after I missed that penalty.

Now, nobody cared much. Whoever turned up was assured of a game, and if you wanted a rest or a cigarette or a can of beer or something to eat you could go off for a while and come back on again. Maybe Chapman was right, after all, and everyone's lack of ambition meant we'd end up as losers. I didn't drink, or smoke, but I could clearly see that a number of half-decent players were already old and useless before their time. I mind once Pilfer, who was the organist at Westminster Abbey, playing for us in a suit and pointed polished shoes after some kind of champagne reception. Drunk as a skunk in goals and somehow managed to save everything that came his way, shouting 'Fortissimo' every time he dived into the mud in his Sunday best to catch the ball. Or perhaps it was Fartissimo. We couldn't quite make it out, for by that time everything was slurred and far away through the mud and rain.

There was no smell of Ralgex or Deep Heat or Brut, for there were no sweaty changing rooms. You either changed in your car or arrived and left in your kit, travelling by public transport. You were always guaranteed a seat for yourself because most folk kept clear.

The School of Pharmacy was in Brunswick Square. I registered on the Foundation Course because I'd been out of the official education system for some years. It was a bit like being back in school again, playing with stuff, and once more charmed by how one thing becomes another, in the same way that a lorry gear could become a bear or a tiger or a panther. Or, I suppose, how a game of football could become all about money. It was easy enough, and good fun to do those elementary experiments once more. Trying to find out how much iron is in Cornflakes by passing a magnet over a few pieces of cereal on the surface of a beaker of water. When that didn't work, I put some cereal into a mortar and used a pestle to produce a fine powder, spread the powder on a piece of paper, and put a magnet under the paper. I moved the paper over the magnet and – well, I wouldn't want to spoil the experiment! It was such fun to discover that if all the iron from your body was extracted, there would be enough for two small nails!

I then progressed to the full four-year pharmacy course. The first two years provided a wide range of options, ranging from cell biology to toxicology. It's always about choices. I'm still not sure how I make them. Or how to live with them once made. That's another choice. When I've had a choice, which has not always been the case. What choice had I to leave the city and move to an island? Or to be in the school I was in, with the classmates I had? Or play well in a football match when a Chelsea coach happened to be around?

Yet so many choices.

It was a frosty February morning. A Friday. We had double maths in the morning, then a break, then a free period. The break ten minutes long and the free period forty minutes. So, fifty minutes all together. And lunch followed, which I could skip. That was another hour. An hour and fifty minutes.

Sally had her skates looped over her shoulders.

'Fancy?'

'Definitely.'

We headed down towards the loch. The path was slippery all the way, so we held hands. Once there, we tested the ice. Small stones first, then large ones. It was frozen solid. Sally was always faster at doing things than I was. She was out skating while I was still tying my laces. She was more daring than I was. Had more courage.

I tied them ever so slowly, because I liked watching Sally skating, and knew that as soon as I went onto the ice she became less free, slowing down so that I could keep up with her. She was skating ever so gracefully, making lines and circles and twirls in the ice. Her speciality was crouching down and then rising slowly on one foot and suddenly reversing direction. I liked the curved marks she made in the ice. She made me feel as if I was doing every twist and turn and rise and fall alongside her as a dance.

I joined her, in my own clumsy way, moving tentatively round the edge of the loch then gradually towards the centre where Sally was skating. We made figures of eight for a while, and then held hands as we moved across the ice. Flakes of snow began to fall, and it was like being inside one of those glass snow globes my Mum collected as paperweights. We raced, Sally moving on one leg, and I bent double trying to catch up with her. After a while I skated over to the side to rest while she continued tracing swirls across the ice.

I removed my tight skates to massage my ankles. That's when I heard a crack in the distance, like a gunshot, and looked up to see the ice coming apart and Sally falling in. For some reason, I didn't make much of it. It wasn't the first time she'd been in the water. We used to swim all the time down at the Otter's Pool and sometimes in the sea itself off the point. I must have thought she'd swim her way out of the water. Never mind it was impossible amid the cold and sheets and lumps of ice around her.

I didn't do anything for ages. It may have been seconds or a whole lifetime. I don't know. The snowflakes kept falling, ever so softly, melting as they landed on my hair and hands and clothes and accumulating further out, where it must have been colder. Where Sally was. Maybe she too was sitting there, flicking the falling snowflakes off the back of her hand and wondering whether she would now skate back or continue on further over to the eastern side, where the swans bedded in the reed banks. But they'd have gone ashore because of the ice.

And I suddenly realised she hadn't surfaced, and because my skates were off I couldn't run across the ice, and by the time I put them on and raced towards her in my own clumsy way it was too late. There was no sign of her, even though I glanced over towards the empty frozen reed bed and the far shore, and I didn't know whether to dive in or not, so I didn't. It's all confusion and chaos and regret and guilt, really, because I think what I did was skate back to the edge, remove my skates and run as fast as I could back to the school to raise the alarm, which I know now, I will know all my life, was stupid and daft and pointless, and what I should have done was to have reached my hand down into the water and hope she caught it, or dive in and pull her up to the surface, or die with her, but instead, I ran away.

Oh, I know everyone has advised and comforted me, saying it wasn't my fault, and that I panicked, and that they wouldn't have known what to do, and at least I didn't do anything foolish and dive in and drown myself too, but those are just words. I should have done better. I could have been with her rather than sitting on the edge massaging my ankles. I could have held on to her as the ice cracked. Been with her right to the end. But I wasn't.

When Sally and I used to sit under the lilac tree, gazing up at the sky, she always said,

'Jack.'

'Aye?'

'See?'

'What?'

'That!'

And she always meant the space between the branches and between the leaves.

'The space.'

'Outer?' I'd say, and she'd laugh and say, 'Inner, Jack. See. The space between.'

The space that is always there. And I'd look and look between the leaves and see… well, at first, I saw nothing, because space, after all, is nothing, isn't it, but then when I really looked – looked properly, I mean – I saw everything. The sky itself, of course, or the clouds or whatever was behind the space, sometimes a bee or a bird or a fly, but I also began to see the space itself. Where she was.

At first I saw edges, mostly leaves, as if the space was where the leaves hadn't yet reached. An absence. As if everything has to be physically seen to be there. But I taught myself to ignore the edges and look at the space itself. As if you could, because time itself alters all space. What I'm seeing now is now what was there a moment ago. All that emptiness which is so full. It's best when you see something in the space, for then you can frame it all round the edges, like a portrait on the wall, so that the space itself is the picture. I suppose that's what all those modern artists like Cezanne did when they began to confuse everyone. Making us see that the mountain we thought was there wasn't a mountain at all. It was just bits and bobs of light and dark.

We must have all done it as children, no? On my seventh birthday Mum made a cake and Dad lit the seven candles so that I could blow them out. Before I blew I sat looking at the candles, then closed one eye and saw the candles flickering to my left, then closed the other eye to see them over to my right, and then when I opened both eyes they were in the middle, as it were. Maybe I understood that it all depended on where you were looking from, or maybe there were three sets of candles, which meant I was twenty-one after all, and could do whatever I pleased. Though I wasn't, for when I blew them out only seven billowed smoke!

Of course, we could see the most sky in the spaces in winter and early spring and late autumn when the leaves had fallen off and the branches were bare, for in the fullness of summer all was leaves and blossoms. Or so it seemed. When we looked closely we always found space, even in and on the leaves themselves, for nothing is solid. Even the leaves and branches and the trunk which looks so whole are full of gaps. It's what keeps them alive.

Sally has always filled the spaces when things were bare. Or when I allowed them to be bare. Football and running and work and memory and chemistry – life – took over, so that at times it seemed like all leaves and blossom and fragrance (even Ralgex!), when in reality it was cold and raw and wintry. It never really mattered that I missed that penalty. It never mattered at all. Though it's there, like the star you see shining on a dark winter's night light years after it's gone.

Space. The final frontier. Where everything connects, as in the Trinity. Time and space and motion. Father, Son, and Holy Ghost. It might even be that's why I liked – or was good at – football. Finding the pockets of space. My career as a chemist has been essentially all about space. The atom is the basic building block of all things, and here's the thing: most of an atom – ninety-nine per cent of it – is empty space. We're more or less nothingness, and if you removed all the empty space contained in every atom in every person on earth and compressed us all together, what's left, all humanity's particles, would be smaller than a sugar cube. We could all sit together beside the teapot in the sugar bowl!

And how we fill that empty space. Watching telly. Waiting for the ferry. Or the bus. For the phone to buzz, the email to arrive. With these words. The leaves and blossoms on the flowers and plants and trees, with all their fragrance hanging in the air.

5

WE HAD TO specialise at the end of the second year. I chose Cosmetic Science. It might seem more noble if I'd chosen something less commercial, or at least medically more useful – Molecular Medicine or Immunology for example – even though nothing isn't commercial. It's all of a scale, like herbal treatments on one hand and medical drugs on the other. And who's to say that looking or smelling nice is not as important as treating acne or corns?

I chose Cosmetic Science because of Sally. Because of our memory of mint, and that seaweedy smell on the seawall where we ran, and the fragrance of blackthorn and hawthorn and dog rose in the maze. The hyacinth smell from her hair when she passed in the school corridor. The word gets such a bad press. Cosmetic, I mean. Standing for something false or fake. External and decorative. But it's the heart of life – the cosmos itself. What we dream and imagine and remember and do. The lovely precision of science, where things need to be exact or they become worthless.

Those football strips we had, blue and white stripes, with blue shorts and white socks and the logo, branding us as a tribe, and the black and white school uniform with the striped tie, and the way we all wore our hair at the time, long, except for those who didn't want to be identified with the group and were Goths, and later in the lab those white coats we all wore, making us scientists. As a child, Jesus made sparrows out of bits of clay. Bit by bit, kneading the wings onto the small body and lining them with his fingernails and then lifting the shape up gently into the air and watching it fly off to freedom.

It's language. The kilt my dad wore on special occasions, such as when he was asked to present the prizes at the local games, and the hat Mum wore to church, and those cloaks the teachers wore, making them ravens in the corridors. And here I am, in my check shirt and chinos, as if I was never a nervous child measuring my height against the wall, or as if I'd never run along the seawall caring about nothing except the stopwatch Sally showed me at the end. One second faster this time, Jack.

It's been about beauty all along. Ever since humans walked the earth and, having caught and eaten, painted their faces and pierced their bodies and scratched the walls to signify that life was more than survival. Look, they said. Look at me. At us, at how different we are from those over the hills and across the river. We have this red mark here and they have that blue mark there. Stripes and circles we have. They use lines and squares. Like Arsenal and Chelsea. Cosmetics was the first language.

I first met Charlotte at a Christmas party. She had a wooden conch-shell earring in her left ear and matching ring on the middle finger of her left hand. She worked in the marketing department of the medical company where I was on placement. She was a bit drunk. We were in a queue to get tags for our bags.

'No one trusts anyone anymore,' she said.

'Never did,' I said. It sounded too smart even then.

I saw her again in the lunch queue on the first day back after the holidays.

'I still have the tag,' she said. 'I couldn't find it at the end of the party, but they gave me my bag anyway. Found it later in my jacket pocket.'

'Shows we didn't need them in the first place.'

'So many things we don't need.'

We sat together and talked. She'd played hockey for a while, but fell in love with skiing on a school trip to Italy years before.

'Never tried it,' I said. 'Maybe it's too much an individual sport for someone spoiled by a team game like football?'

'I doubt it,' she said. 'The slope is a great collective, weaving and slaloming past one another.'

I saw Sally waltzing gracefully across the ice.

'I must try it,' I said.

We never say the things we mean to say.

Our first date was the following week, after work on Friday. At the local pub round the corner.

'So?'

'So. Cheers!'

She drank gin and I had a whisky. They didn't have any malt, which might have made a sip possible, so I accepted what they had. Johnston's. Even the smell was rubbish, which gave me a good excuse not to touch it at all. I should have known the signs. But maybe we see what we want to see and ignore what we don't anyway. And it takes such a long time to see patterns. Waves, billows, stripes, lines, curves, squares. Always there, obscured by activity.

'I'm going to Austria to ski last weekend of the month. The long weekend.'

'Can I come too?'

'You'll learn,' she said.

And I did. It was strange being in a place where it was warm yet covered in snow. Down in the villages we walked about in light clothing while up on the slopes all we added were our jerseys, helmets, and skis. It was like going from the fireside out into the fresh air on an autumn day at home. And maybe that's how I forgot about the ice, for the snow was soft and fluffy, and when I fell into it countless times on the learners' lower slopes it was like rolling in a downie. And then suddenly, when I took the gondola up to a higher slope, I saw the ice forming on a lake further down the valley, and there was Sally again, her skates swinging over her neck. She tied them on ever so swiftly and headed off across the ice in loops and twirls and turns and skips and jumps, the skates leaving deep marks behind her as she moved across the ice, turning at the north end where the small canopy of pine trees glittered in the frost and as she turned it was Charlotte, skiing downhill ever so fast away from the gondola and I watched her crouch down low before straightening up again and jumping in a spectacular somersault, landing safely and speeding downhill, her silver helmet glistening in the sun. She made me afraid.

I followed on my first downhill run. It was only from the first stop, though it was pretty terrifying nevertheless. All your life you've learned to lean into the solid security of a surface, lying in your mother or lover's arms, and there on the slope your instructor's voice in your head tells you to lean away from the mountain while every sinew in your body strains towards it. And then the moment when it happens. You let go, and turn, not because you've done anything special but because you've let – oh, I don't know what it is – gravity or instinct or liberty or nature or something do its stuff, and next thing I was skiing downhill, remembering to bend the knees this way and that, and it was like seeing myself on film being something I never felt – elegant. And then I crashed to a stop at the bottom, because I'd forgotten how to do that snowplough thing, but the snow was thick and soft and fluffy anyway and I lay there laughing, now that I was safe.

We stayed in one of the self-catering chalets with a picture window looking onto the Alps. In the moonlight we could see coloured figures skiing down the slopes. I thought of Fitzgerald and careless lives. Destroyed by money and leisure and bourbon. Sometimes Dad smelled of drink – whisky – and Mum was forever furtively checking nooks and crannies for glasses and bottles. Yet he was never drunk, and always pleasant and considerate. Maybe that memory warned me. Charlotte opened a bottle of wine.

'Sure?' she said.

'Completely.'

'A glass won't do any harm.'

'I know. But two will. Or three. Or four…'

'You can stop at one.'

'That's like saying you can stop skiing after one slalom. You have to keep going. Downhill.'

She laughed.

'No you don't. You're in control of this bottle, not gravity. Anyway. Why?'

'I don't like the taste. Makes me sick.'

'But you don't mind…?'

'No. Go ahead.'

Liar, I said to myself. Of course I minded. I don't know where it came from, this puritan streak in me. I hate to see good things going to waste. Football was always destroyed for me by bawling and shouting. Like beating a beautiful dog with a stick. I always thought it should be more of a dance – a ballet. Players elegantly moving themselves and the ball around the pitch, but instead it invariably became a shouting match. Not among the spectators but from my teammates. My colleagues, who should instinctively know, and trust, what was happening.

'Jack! Jack, Jack! Pass,' they'd shout, as if I didn't know where they all were and where the ball should go. It should have been like guddling barefoot in a stream for cuddies.

Maybe that's what lay behind that penalty incident. Not just the cheating, but the spoiling of a good and fair thing. You take your chance and sometimes it works out, sometimes it doesn't. No doubt it came from my childhood. My mother's obsession with neatness and tidiness, perhaps, so that I was always aware that the books on the shelf should be in alphabetical order, and that the forks should be in this cutlery drawer and the fish knives in that one and the teaspoons here and the soup spoons there and so on.

And nothing should go to waste. Of course it shouldn't. People throw out perfectly good food which they could use to make soup and freeze. Perfectly good chairs and stools and cupboards litter the streets. But above all the waste of lives. Destroyed by one thing or another. Drink, wealth, poverty, greed, hopelessness. Dad never felt good enough. I didn't know that in the early days, for he was The Headie, and everyone looked up to him and jumped at his commands. But he shared more when he retired and had the chance to come to London. He'd travel on the pretence of seeing some of our Sunday matches, though it was really to go to the British Library and the British Museum and the Victoria and Albert. His favourite was the Petrie Museum of Egyptian Archaeology where he spent hours showing me pyramid texts and ancient tools and rods and mirrors. Those were the days when museum collections tended to be guarded away behind glass and in boxes and cases, but the Egyptian Museum was so different, because you could actually handle the stones and scrolls – or at least perfect copies of them – and Dad was ever so keen to use the red carbon copy paper which he could place over the stones and scrolls to trace out the letters and hieroglyphs. In one room we were given small hammers and chisels and, under supervision from a carving expert, allowed to carve our own names into stone.

Beyond the museums, Dad seemed disappointed to see so many new buildings in London.

'I hoped it would be more Dickensian,' he said.

We were standing on Westminster Bridge looking west in the early morning.

'Let it always be like this,' he said.

It was such a strange, almost poetic, thing for him to say. Normally he only referred to the physical, like the boats moving up and down the river.

'For you,' he added. 'Jack.'

He so rarely used my name.

'Breakfast?' he added.

We went to The River Café and had the full English.

'I don't know if you ever read the Bible nowadays?' he said.

'Not really. Just bits and pieces now and again. The poetry of the psalms. He makes me down to lie, in pastures green he leadeth me the quiet waters by.'

'There's a bit in the book of Acts,' he said. 'When the two are walking back to Emmaus. And then this stranger joins them and they talk about everything that happened in Jerusalem and they say, "We had hoped." It's the most powerful bit in the whole Bible. We had hoped, Jack.'

After breakfast I went off to do some light training

and left Dad to see the sights. He liked taking the river boats and usually went out to Greenwich to see the Cutty Sark. He never tired of going on board, caressing the hull, walking around the cargo deck, having a look inside the Captain's Cabin, with its solid oak furniture and brass nautical instruments. I don't know what happens now, but in those days you could pick up a cloth and polish the glass and the brass. Dad spent some time shining in slow circles. Those who were there say he then, without warning and despite all the rules, began climbing the rigging and, once up at the topsail yard, slipped and fell.

I've read that bit in the Book of Acts since, and know what they hoped for: the thing that they already had. The man who was walking with them, unknown to them. Dad has walked with me ever since. I don't know who didn't walk with him. Mum, maybe. Hoping that she would hold him as he walked, though it was impossible because he was so far away. I remember as a wee boy walking behind them. Mum reached out her hand to hold his and he immediately put it into his pocket. I thought it was unfair. I ran up and held Mam's hand instead.

Charlotte bought some bottles of wine and got blind drunk that night, and eventually passed out on the sofa. In the morning, I made strong coffee for both of us.

'Shall we walk rather than ski today?'

'Sure. My head would cope better with that.'

The snow was solid and crisp under our feet. The walk took us from the chalet down towards the forest track which had hardly any snow, except in the treetops. We could smell the citrusy scent of larch and the unmistakable resin of pine.

'O my God, that's the best hangover cure ever,' she said as we inhaled the forest air.

We brought a picnic lunch. Bread and cheese and tomatoes and a small jar of local honey. And water. We sat by a stream to have it. I suppose it was an attempt to get away from ourselves. Maybe that's what nature always is. It does not envy or boast. I was going to say that it keeps no record of wrongs, but of course it does. It weeps and mourns from all the damage we've done to it and the scars we've made on it. And yet, as we sat there by the stream, in the stillness, enveloped by the smells of the forest, it made no accusation and didn't blame us for anything. It was the sound of a Sabbath. Maybe it praised us for sitting there in the silence. I emptied my bottled water and replaced it with fresh water from the stream.

'If only,' Charlotte said. 'If only.'

We lay on our backs looking up at the clear blue sky. It was so much clearer and bluer than the sky in Scotland. As if it had never had to deal with wind and rain. Charlotte spoke. Talked about her childhood in the Chilterns.

'We went to Scotland on holiday once, when I was about ten, and only then realised how flat our hills were. We went hillwalking every weekend. Mum and Dad and Sophie and Lucy and John and I. Full of chalk streams and rivers. And the salt marshes. They were lovely. We also liked wandering about the quarries. Mum and Dad have retired now to the Lake District.'

'And picnics,' she said. 'There's something special about them.'

She sat up leaning on one elbow.

'The Sunday school picnic was the best ever. At Coombe Hill. We had three picnics in one. Bacon rolls and tea for breakfast. Then sandwiches and lemonade at the top of the hill. And then cakes and sweeties after we came down. Cinnamon rolls and lemon muffins and maple-walnut sticky buns. But the thing I remember most is that we all sang at the top of the hill. "We Have an Anchor" led by Canon Roberston. Which was strange because we couldn't see the sea, but everyone stood to sing it and the wind was blowing ever so strong and because of that we must all have raised our voices and it was as if we were fighting and beating the storm all around us.'

She stood up and began singing. Maybe it was the stillness of the day and the nearness of the trees and the clarity of the sky but it was as if she was a choir, each word and syllable echoing and re-echoing in perfect harmony through the woods.

> Will your anchor hold in the storms of life?
> When the clouds unfold their wings of strife,
> When the strong tides lift, and the cables strain,
> Will your anchor drift or firm remain.

And I too went back to Sunday school and lay there singing,

> We have an anchor that keeps the soul,
> Steadfast and sure while the billows roll,
> Fastened to the Rock which cannot move,
> Grounded firm and deep in the Saviour's love.

And there was Dad in the third pew from the right singing it in that long slow way of his with Mum by his side chivvying him on to hurry up so that his words could keep up with the music, played on the old organ by Mrs Scott. The organ wheezed between every second note, giving Dad a chance to catch up.

He once gave me a top tip. 'Jack,' he said. 'See anytime you go to church – in fact to any public event – make sure you always sit beside the oldest woman in the building. Then cough a little, and she'll immediately feed you with Mint Imperials from that bottomless bag of hers until the final sung Amen.'

It's true.

Charlotte sat back down beside me.

'I wonder if we could make this our fragrance?' she said, after a while.

It was the tangy pitchy fragrance of pine blended with the citrus of larch.

'We could. Maybe we already are. All things are possible.'

'It's strange,' she said then. 'That we're in this business.'

'No stranger than any other.'

'I mean in the sense that here it all is, and we try to capture and sell it. Steal it.'

'It's no one's, so why not? It's like memory, isn't it? Ours – yours and mine – as much as anyone else who's ever been here.'

'But commercialised? Is that what it's about?'

'Perfume? Smelling nice. About attracting girls. Boys. About feeling good. Covering up body odours. Making money. You know all that. You market it, after all.'

She sat up.

'I think it's about something much more important.'

'Tell me.'

She lay on top of me and kissed me. She tasted of honey.

'It's about telling ourselves that we're more than our bodies. That we can be trees and rivers and mountains and snow and ocean and sky and everything. That there are no limits to what we can be.'

'But there are.'

She pulled away and stood up. How could I say it? Well. Sally, and Mum and Dad, and Geordie Smith and Mr Chapman and me and Charlotte with all our weaknesses and follies. Her drinking. That white powder dust around her place. Maybe I'd never grown bigger than the highest pencil mark on the window frame. Missed penalties and opportunities. Sitting there tying my laces. Dad unable to say he loved me. Geordie Smith always at the sweets counter then immediately heading for the chip shop as soon as school closed. Chapman, endlessly smoking, as he tried to gauge the next bet. What if we become what we do, rather than what we imagine we are?

'Don't take things so seriously, Jack. So seriously. It's just a game,' he always said. 'Just a game. Means nothing at the end of the day, nothing at all, so why not get some benefit out of it? Something out of it for yourself!'

But what about all those other beautiful things that had defied the limits? The time Sally raced round the seawall in record time, without cheating. When we lay in the maze smelling the buddleia and wild garlic and lilacs. Somehow they smelt of truth and courage and faithfulness and honesty. When we kissed in the pouring rain as we waited for the school bus, delayed by the floods. We tried to dry each other's faces before the bus arrived. The astonishing goal I scored against Crystal Palace, skipping past six players and hitting the ball into the postage-stamp corner. The way Charlotte stood, her hair shining gold in the sun, as if all the pine trees around, with their glistening frosty branches, were her handmaidens.

She was right, after all.

6

WHEN WE GOT back to London we decided on a partnership. Our own small cosmetics company. We called it Larch and Pine. It's a bit strange to recall that the organic market had not yet taken off, so we were unique in that sense at the time, promising to only use sustainable, non-animal, natural products. I don't think that was quite the language we used then – we named things after the main scent – but that's what they were.

It was tough at first, of course. The two of us and a big bank loan with which we rented premises in South Norwood next to Elmers End station. The loan also enabled us to hire three other workers – Dr Elise Carthwood, who left Unilever to join us for 'ethical reasons', my college chemistry tutor Shava Bhansali, and Irene Wilson, newly graduated from Cambridge in Ecology and who answered our advert for a qualified scientist interested in developing homeopathic scents and perfumes.

They were heady, adventurous days, verging on bankruptcy most of the time, but able to survive thanks to the old-fashioned Mr Davidson who ran the bank in

Croydon. He always wore a pinstriped suit and a yellow dotted bow tie.

'Ah! A cottage industry,' he said to us at the first meeting. 'My favourite part of the job – supporting all these local little makers without whom the country would not survive. The nation of small shopkeepers. But there must be precision. Without precision, what's science or engineering?'

Charlotte's mother was French, which made a useful impression on him.

'Ah, Les français! La France! Le peuple que je préfère! L'endroit que je préfère! Ce que ces héros ont fait pour moi!'

He stood and went over to the cupboard to pour us each a brandy.

'And you're Scotch?' he said.

I hesitated to correct him, seeing we were in need.

'Scottish. Scotch is the drink.'

'Slàinte,' he said, taking a gulp of his brandy. 'My grandmother was Scottish. From Argyll. Barbreck. Just testing you!'

He was a fascinating character and became a sort of unpaid advisor and sleeping partner in the business. Partially because of his business knowledge, but also because of his keen interest in folk medicine. After a while he loosened up. The brandy helped, the way it helps some people. As he heard about our desire to develop homeopathic perfumes, he began to tell us about his mother's interest in folk remedies. Eventually he gave us access to his family's unique collection of traditional recipes and cures from Argyll and his own native Sussex.

'Look,' he said, after that first meeting. 'These are some of my mother's notes.'

The brown paper-lined school jotter lay on his desk alongside some financial reports and spreadsheets.

'To cure a hangover. Take a bunch of Sea Pinks pulled with the roots. Boil for an hour or more. Leave to cool. Drink slowly, and you're ready for another night ashore. That's what all the sailors said anyway. You could maybe patent that?' Davidson said. 'Or how about this?' he continued. 'For indigestion – find fresh dulse from the shore and eat it raw. Or boil the entire plant of Tormentil and drink the juice. Also boil nettle tops and drink the juice. That will cure any stomach trouble.'

'Anything there about perfumes, though?' I asked.

He opened another jotter covered with coloured and speckled paper.

'Take sweet marjoram, thyme, lavender, rosemary, pennyroyal buds, red roses, violet flowers, clove July-flowers, savoury, and orange peels of each equal parts; infuse in white wine until everything sinks entirely to the bottom; then distil in an alembic two or three times. Keep the water in bottles well corked and preserve the residuum as a perfume.'

We wondered where we would get all those ingredients, and later, once we were in profit, hired a gardener to grow them for us.

When he died, Davidson bequeathed his mother's

jotters to us, and these days I spend quiet evenings reading through them, comforting myself with old knowledge and superstitions that would heal the world.

Despite Davidson's help, we barely survived as a business. One day we held a crisis meeting. Davidson chaired it and presented what he called the clear options: to close and go bankrupt, or make a deal with Unilever, who were interested in developing the organic market and had already bought out quite a few small companies like ours here and there.

'I know the gentlemen who run the company, and I'm sure we can negotiate a deal which will please both you and them.'

We had two options, he said. We could sell the whole business, its identity, products, and staff to them, or negotiate a percentage for ourselves.

'Say they owned fifty or seventy-five per cent, with all the muscle that would bring with it, and you would still have a say – fifty or twenty-five or whatever per cent – in how the new company operates.'

Charlotte and I owned the business between us, but I wanted Dr Carthwood and Shava and Irene to have their say as founding members of the venture. We agreed on a secret vote, with Davidson excluding himself, and the vote went three–two to make a deal with Unilever. I voted against, and I still don't know, because I never asked, who voted the other way. Except for Charlotte, who told me she voted to work with Unilever.

'That way we can influence what happens without the full risk. We can dance with the devil, as it were.'

Except you can't. You can choose the instruments and the music, but the devil plays the tune and leads the dance. Takes what he wants when he wants. When I was wee, in Sunday school, we read an illustrated book about the time Jesus was in the desert and the devil came to tempt him. In the first drawing, when he tempted Jesus to turn stones into bread, the devil was a big fat baker. In the second one, when Jesus was tempted to throw himself off the pinnacle of the temple, the devil was a man wearing a parachute, holding a big bouncing mattress waiting for Jesus to jump, and in the third illustration, when Jesus is shown all the kingdoms of this world, the devil was a clown with balloons and candy and toys on a cart telling Jesus to come down and buy. I always knew that the devil didn't go round the world with horns and a tail and with smoke coming out of his nostrils and backside. He appeared as an angel of light.

Was I the angel of light? Selling potions to the world. Musk and lavender and cinnamon and bergamot to sweeten all those little hands. Who doesn't need to live? Who doesn't want to smell nice and look pretty and be what you want to be, even if it means throwing yourself off the top of some temple, seeing a bouncy mattress waiting for you anyway, where you can somersault and do a pirouette and bow to the crowd?

So we traded for a while, on a seventy-five per cent (for them) and twenty-five per cent (for us) agreement.

'A quarter of the risk for you,' Carter said, 'so a quarter of the rewards. Fair's fair, eh?'

And it was. Our quarter job was to source indigenous ingredients, while Unilever's team processed and sold the products far and wide.

'Of course they'll adulterate the ingredients,' I said.

'So?' Charlotte said.

'Means it will be neither organic nor natural.'

'What is?'

'As it is.'

'So just leave it there, Jack? Leave the cloves on the tree and the mint in the ground and spring water in the spring? Go naked while you're at it.'

I raised the issue with Carter, who was in charge of processing and selling the perfumes.

'I thought you were a chemist?' he said in response. 'Isn't that what chemistry is – taking a thing and turning it into something else? Or music or storytelling or drawing or football or anything. Isn't that what life is? Taking things as they are and turning them into something of value?'

'Not by destroying them.'

'We only add fixatives. Glycerine, limonene, and so on. But you know that anyway. Same as you take a paracetamol when you've got a headache.'

'Raspberry tea does the same job.'

'Okay. Well, you sell that then, and make your fortune.'

It was tempting. I hung in for a while. Not because I was a saint, but because everything is worth a try. Despite those childish pictures of the devil, maybe he could be cheated, danced out the door? Maybe he wasn't as bad as he'd been painted anyway. Maybe he didn't exist. What was temptation but my own desire and greed and ambition? My desire for bread from stone. My greed for fame. My ambition to be someone, have wealth, own the world. Chapman was wrong. Oh, I had my ambitions all right – just not his. The ambition to be decent. To be fair and good and kind and true. To distinguish right from wrong. To do my best. Knowing that I hadn't always, and had failed so miserably. I could have stayed on that First XI if I'd always given it my all. If I'd really wanted to. I could have... If only, as Charlotte had put it. If only. But there was always now.

I went round negotiating with farmers and smallholders who grew organic stuff. Little farms in Wales and Ireland and a haven in Wiltshire run by Mrs Whitlock and her daughters and some cooperatives in France and Spain who supplied us with enough laurel and thyme and rosemary and sweet marjoram and lavender and sage and mint and hyssop and anise and fennel to get by. But even then it was never enough. When a thing becomes industrialised and commercialised it becomes insatiable, like a wild beast. It needs to be increasingly enhanced by chemicals to sustain production for a growing market. That, or diluted, which is the same form of destruction, cheating the herbs as well as the customers out of their essence.

I can spot diluted perfume a mile away. It has that insipid watery look, even inside a beautiful glazed bottle. It's a lie concealed between smart words and advertising. And it always fails the sniff test: when you open the fake bottle it's instantly too sweet. The real perfume takes its time to approach you, the way the grass smells when you open the window after a sudden summer rainfall.

Patterns. England's green and pleasant land, packed like squares of wheat as you fly over it. Scotland's rivers running like veins down the mountainsides. How cricketers shape themselves in the field, angling to catch that arcing ball. The way children instinctively skip when they see chalk marks on the ground. And Charlotte, with that excitable nervous energy when she planned to go out drinking, and her anxiety during withdrawal, and the secrecy surrounding her other vices, all like waves of the ocean coming and going with the tides, or like the roughly woven patterns in her Harris Tweed caps.

And how can you confront anyone with their behaviour when you know full well your own weaknesses and foibles and follies? Those soft snowflakes falling and melting on my clothes and the ice cracking and the swans all silent in the empty reed beds, and the terrible stillness all around as I stood there. How fragile we are. And what if I was wrong, which is what she claimed anyway, for I had no proof except my instinct, and what kind of proof is that? It's like saying the moon is made of cheese because it's got holes in it. So I stopped saying anything, like the man who pretended to be deaf when the bear roared and blind when the light was switched on.

Who can help us in times of need? We made promises

to each other. I would chum her to places where she felt vulnerable. She wouldn't drink secretly. We went to AA together, and she went to see a counsellor and finally went into a rehab centre out in the country. Then one day she said, 'Jack, you know what? I actually don't want to be sober. I like it.'

'No you don't. You hate it.'

'Only at its worst point.'

'It's always at its worst point. That first gin is as bad as the last.'

'How would you know. That first snort is great. And the second and the third…'

It was too early. Maybe I didn't have enough patience and Charlotte wasn't yet ready. It was a pretty messy end, with the business part of it all tangled up with our personal lives. I sold my shares to Unilever. Charlotte kept hers for a while, but she too cashed in some months later. She got clean a couple of years after that and moved to Ireland where she set up a holistic medicine and yoga practice. She still went skiing once a year. Part of our Christmas ritual was for her to send me a good old-fashioned postcard from Austria, while I sent her yet another postcard with a picture of the Caledonian MacBrayne ferry from Mull sailing in past Rubh' A' Bheàrnaig into Oban Bay.

7

I WENT HOME for Dad's funeral, and never went back to London. There had been an official inquest, which took a while, and concluded that it had been an accident. A lawyer tried to persuade us to take the Cutty Sark people to court under health and safety rules, but neither Mum nor I wanted to do that. What purpose would it serve, except to rake up things and make people feel bad? For what – money? And the ship was as safe as any other if you wanted to take care.

Back home, Mum was the same as ever, organising everything and putting the house in order. The funeral service was held in the remaining local church. I'd forgotten how comforting it was to sing the unaccompanied psalms, unspoilt by organ or any other musical instrument. Just us and the words.

The internment was in the old cemetery on the hill. It was a windy day. Our voices carried across the water as we laid the coffin into the grave, singing Psalm 16 to the tune of Cunningham:

> I love the Lord, because my voice
> and prayers he did hear.

I, while I live, will call on him,
who bowed to me his ear.

Of death the cords and sorrows did
about me compass round;
The pains of hell took hold on me,
I grief and trouble found.

Upon the name of God the Lord
then did I call, and say,
Deliver thou my soul, O Lord,
I do thee humbly pray.

It's wonderfully comforting when a thing rhymes. All seems well with the world, capable of being fixed and put in order.

We had soup and bread and tea in the local hall. So many people came up to me and talked. I didn't know who they were. For a while I nodded and accepted their sympathy, before I realised I could simply be honest and shake my head and say, 'Sorry, I can't remember…' and then they'd always fill in the rest and tell me not to apologise, for it had been such a long time, and my father had been so good to their children when he was running the school, and then some of the children themselves, now adults, came up and shook my hand and said how kind my father had been to them, for instance that time Don and James shattered the school window with a ball and all Dad had done was thank them for telling him and, anyway, how splendid it was that they spent their playtime with a football rather than hanging about the school shelter.

Back home, Mum wasted no time in removing Dad's clothes and things from the cupboards.

'They can't stay there gathering dust and moths. It's not what he would have wanted. And they will do someone a turn.'

So she organised an open garden day and I've no doubt the whole thing helped us to grieve as we put his suits and shirts and shoes and ties and cufflinks – so many, and they were all so lovely – and all the rest of his stuff on railings and in order on various tables, except for his desk, which sat still untouched in the house. She had checked the weather forecast and Saturday promised to be a good dry sunny day with a slight breeze from the west. And so it was.

She asked me to gather some flowers and shells to decorate the tables we laid out in the garden. When folk from all around arrived it was more like a Spring Festival than a funeral roup. Dad's clothes and things were all free, except we put out a charity box for the local WRI (as it was then) which Mum was President of that year. All the money then went to causes such as the Old Folk's Christmas lunch and to buy flowers and gifts and seats for the local eventide home and so on.

After the sale, Mum and I went back to what felt like an emptied home. It was still full of our beds and cupboards and clothes and furniture and pictures and books and ornaments and all the rest: just that Dad's coat wasn't hanging at the back of the door, and his shoes were not on the rack, and the smell of his tobacco and clay pipe was fainter than it had been even the day before. Mum made tea in the good pot and brought out the china cups, which is what you do at times like these.

She gestured to me to sit in Dad's chair.

'Otherwise it will sit there empty,' she said, 'with everyone afraid to sit in it.'

It was lovely, and when I leant into it the back moved with me and settled around my posture.

I never really knew my mother until then. Oh, of course I'd known her as my Mum. She always put food on the table. The potatoes always on the right-hand side of the plate. The fish or meat towards me or in the middle, and the veg always on the left-hand side. Sometimes cabbage, sometimes peas, sometimes simple lettuce and tomato. She always washed my school clothes on Saturday and then ironed them on Sunday afternoon or evening, ready for school on Monday.

But I never knew her as a woman. As someone who had hopes and fears and desires and anxieties and ambitions. When she picked wild flowers and put them in vases around the house it never crossed my mind that the lilies or bluebells or bell heather or whatever would remind her of the days of her childhood playing with her three sisters down by the stream near Kelvingrove. Or that when she spent a morning making scones or bread or cakes in the big oven she'd be seeing her own mother and granny doing the same all those years ago in their tenement kitchen.

'Isn't it strange,' she said, 'that there are so few green

flowers? I suppose that's because the leaves want that colour for themselves?'

So that first evening of the funeral roup we began to know one another. She asked me to fetch out the photo albums and we looked through them together. There she was as a child pushing a pram with a dolly in it down a street in Glasgow, and here she was on her first day at school with a white ribbon in her hair.

'Mam was ever so proud,' she said. 'Said I was the bonniest lassie in the whole world.'

And there she was on a bicycle, standing with another lassie, somewhere near Loch Lomond.

'That's my best pal, Jessie,' she said. 'She became a nurse and emigrated to Canada. I still have all her letters she sent me in the drawer.'

'I remember the air-mail letters,' I said. 'They had such bonnie stamps. I collected them for a while.'

'So you did. So you did,' she said. 'Do you still have them?'

'Aye. They're probably in one of the drawers in my bedroom.'

And I did, for I looked them out later that night once Mum had gone to bed. All those beautiful stamps of Lake Erie and Lake Huron and Lake Superior and of Air Canada and the Niagara Falls and my favourite one when I was a child, of the Calgary Stampede. It was such an action-filled stamp, with three cowboys – that would have been me and Sparky and Sid – reining in a big white horse bucking up on its hind legs. It took us days to tame it, but we always managed in the end, as we ran, leaping walls and ditches and whole rivers, over the hill.

The other album was of a slightly older Mum. Pictures of her at Glasgow College of Art where she was a student and where she met Dad at a dance. At the time he was at Jordanhill College of Education training to be a teacher. Photographs of Dad on his weekend expeditions as a Scout leader. Map reading in an empty glen, carrying an ice-axe on a snowy crevice in Glencoe, up to his knees in water exploring some underground cave. Living in another world for a while. Then pictures of them both on a motorbike – Dad driving and Mum in the sidecar – down in the Borders and in Ayrshire and up around Blair Atholl, and then photographs of their wedding and of me as a wee baby in a pram and sitting in the sand by the sea. 'Troon' it said on the back of the picture.

And then Mum brought down a book of cuttings from her room one night. All those scissored-out news items from the local paper about Dad and about the WRI – their annual visits out to Iona Abbey – and then the cuttings from the local and national papers about my football career. 'Local lad scores hat-trick!' 'Local boy signs for Chelsea!' and all those grainy pictures I'd never seen, or had forgotten about, scoring a goal at Stamford Bridge and picking up a medal at Wembley and signing forms with sharp-suited agents and track-suited managers in wood-panelled offices somewhere down south. It's always different from how you imagined it would be.

'Your Dad was ever so proud,' she said.

And then. There they were. The cuttings from the local paper about Sally. Tragic incident. Tragic accident. Enquiry to follow. School and community mourn local girl.

'I don't think you ever read them,' Mum said. 'And you don't have to read them now. I'd forgotten they were there. Didn't mean to expose you to them. I know how close you were.'

She lifted the albums to carry them back to her room.

'No,' I said. 'Leave them.'

She did. She went through to the kitchen. I could hear her singing as she washed the dishes and began preparing the porridge for the morning.

'Morning has broken,' she sang. 'Like the first morning. Blackbird has spoken, like the first bird…'

I couldn't help myself and joined in, pleased she could also hear me through the closed kitchen door, 'Praise for the singing! Praise for the morning! Praise for them springing, fresh from the word.'

Sally's picture in the papers was in black and white, though I always saw her in colour. Her fair hair. The green shamrock bangle she wore over her left wrist. The blue blouse she wore in summer and the white sandshoes, as we called them in those days. The photograph was the official one the school must have given, of her in her school uniform, all neat and tidy with her long hair tied back and the school badge with its image of a griffin and the motto Per Ardua ad Astra on her lapel.

Mum came back through with two mugs of tea and

a plate of Tunnock's Tea Cakes. They were my favourite as a teenager.

'It broke my heart too,' she said. 'Although I never said. I knew how fond you were of each other. Always did. Always were.'

She paused.

'You never get over it.'

'Me too,' she continued. 'I had a boyfriend. Before I met your dad. Samuel. Sammy. We did everything together. Just goofing around, I suppose, but still together. Roller-skating was the big thing at the time, and I mind Sammy got these flashy new ones from some auntie of his and he was forever showing off in them. Twirls and turns and loops and jumps and everything. But he took it too far. First on top of garden walls, then on shed and garage roofs and then onto the tops of buildings. We all warned him. I told him it was far too scary and risky. Then one day, and I suppose he wanted to show off to me, we climbed up the back fire escape of this office building and he began to do those leaps like you sometimes see at the Olympics and I don't know exactly what happened but the next thing he slipped and couldn't control the skates and hit the bollard fence at the edge, and…'

She caressed the mug of tea, as if warming her hands.

'… and, when I heard about Sally, well then, I was back there too, all angry and tearful and confused, but I didn't say anything to you at the time because I didn't want you to think I was being smart and a know-all, and lessening your grief by saying that I too had gone through the same, for all our pains and sorrows and anguish are always unique, no matter how much others say they understand... no matter the terrible longing we all have for clear answers...'

I'm not sure I took it all in at the time. It was so strange. This woman – my mother, Mum – talking in this calm, mature way as if I wasn't her wee boy or teenage lad or distant son anymore, but what I was, a man after her own image who could look at things calmly and with reason. So she too had suffered, and borne it.

'And I loved your father.'

She laughed, as if she was a young woman again, astonished by the uniqueness of things.

'Your tea's getting cold,' she said. 'Drink it while it's hot.'

I took a sip.

'We met at the union dance,' she said. 'He was ever so shy. Old-fashioned in many ways. I may have imagined it, but I think he even bowed when he asked me to dance. And not for fun or anything, but because he thought that's the way things ought to be done. Manners, he called it afterwards. Though he was as stubborn as a rock. You needed dynamite to move him once he made his mind up, and I could never be bothered with the damage those explosions caused. I should have led him, like a child, more often. It would have done us both the world of good."

She talked a lot that night. About Dad and his ways and his old-fashioned courtesies and the concerts they went to – her favourite one was the time Tony Bennett played at the Kelvin Hall and they had a front row seat and sang and crooned to every song. And I never knew that she knew them all as she sat there singing one after the other: 'Fly Me to the Moon', 'Love Is Here to Stay', 'Yesterday I Heard the Rain', 'The Shadow of Your Smile', and her all-time favourite, 'I Left My Heart in San Francisco'.

'I always wanted to go there, to see the little cable cars, but your dad had a great fear of flying so we never got there.'

Fear. What a terrible thing it is. After Mum went to bed, I stayed up for a good while in the silence. I could hear the sea, far off, swishing against the wall where Sally and I used to run. I put on my coat and went out. It was a clear, chilly night. Strange how you see only a few stars at first, then more and more and more, as if they weren't there to begin with, but then decide to come out because it's safe and the skies are clear and polished and they know you are there, looking up and admiring them as they shine and glow and glitter. Counting them too sometimes.

It's easy at first, The Plough with its seven stars and then the big bright one of Polaris and the five of Cassiopeia, and if you look the other way Rigel and the Belt of Orion and Betelgeuse, so that's twenty so far and you don't know the name of any of the others but there they are shining bright as if to say 'Look at me' and 'What about me?' and 'Me too', and then you get lost in the magnitude and wonder of it all, there you are alive and Mum is safe in her bed and you see the moon shining on the graveyard up on the hill and you think, 'Aye, I'll do it. Even if it's the middle of the night and this is the time the ghosts and bogles wander all through the world, I'll go and confront them all and stand firm and scare them away.' And you think, 'What if they're just as frightened as I am? They want me, or you or Geordie Smith or Chapman or Dad or anyone, to be there with them so that they won't be scared stiff either?'

So I walked along by the sea wall and up the hill track to where the cemetery lay shining in the moonlight, all the gravestones standing to attention, except for the very old ones which lay down flat here and there forgotten in the uncut grass. I saw names as I walked through and by and over them, John dearly beloved and Ann wife of and born 1872 and sorely missed and Fois agus Sìth until the dawn breaks and there she was. Sally Henderson. With her date of birth and date of death and Beloved Daughter and the bridge-shaped moon shining down on the small cross incised above her name and I went on my knees and because all the stars in the universe were weeping with me I thanked her for everything she meant to me and the way she ran across the wall and the way she never cheated or called me out for the time I did take that shortcut round the back of the seawall which I wanted to confess to her but didn't because I thought telling her would be even worse than doing it so I didn't and it remained there inside me all those years like a cracked vase leaking water and thanked her for being my chum and sitting beside me in geography class and for asking me to join her that day she went skating and how beautifully she moved and I told her I could still see the arcs and loops and curves and twirls and circles she left on the ice and I said I was sorry I couldn't save her and she said that's okay because it was the greatest day of her life and she remembered how frosty it was that morning which is why she'd taken her skates with her and how she'd suffered for two hours in the double maths period waiting for the break and the free period and it just so happened that she saw me as she was on her way to the loch and was so glad I joined her so I could see how good she was at skating and it was just one of those things, the ice cracking and breaking, same as everything else that happens, good bad or indifferent, and what matters is that we lay side by side in the maze garden and smelt the lilacs and buddleia and we had all that fun together and wasn't it a beautiful night, Jack, and did you see all those stars and did you hear the sea waves crashing against our wall and why don't you run it tomorrow as we did, I'm sure you're still fit enough to do that, what with all that training you did down south all those years while I rested here listening to the wind in the trees and waiting for you to come and say, hallo, I love you.

The orange light of dawn rose in the east over towards the mainland. The snowy hilltops were already flashing. Out beyond us in the Minch I could hear the soft throb of fishing engines on their way to the Garvellachs and beyond with their creels. All the gravestones began to cast off their dew. As I walked through and past and over them all, I paused at each one to read the names and dates and blessings until I reached my father's still unstoned grave. Again I knelt to thank him for bringing us here. What was there to fear while they were all still blethering away despite the night and dark and holy silence? What was there to forgive?

Mum was up and stirring the porridge when I got home.

'Ah,' she said. 'There you are. I'll put the breakfast out.'

And the table was set so beautifully. Two plates and side-plates and the silver toast-rack and the milk jug and sugar and the coffee pot steaming on the mobile hot plate set in the middle of the table.

'What a beautiful night,' she said. 'I stayed up for a while watching the stars.'

'Me too,' I said.

'Are you planning to stay on?'

I lifted the coffee pot and poured her a cup.

'Where else would I get coffee like this?'

'There's a house for sale along in the village. One of the fisher cottages.'

'Aye, I saw,' I said.

It was old Johnny's. I remembered him from my childhood. He smelt of fish and seaweed, and folk used to hold their noses as they passed his house, as if that would make him change his ways. He always sat on a wooden stool outside most of the day and on warm summer evenings. I never minded the smell and nor did Sally, and we sometimes wandered over to his house to show him we didn't care. Though it wasn't really to see him, but to see the whole menagerie of animals he kept about the house and in his various sheds and outhouses. Ducks and hens and geese and quails and turkeys and our favourites – Billy and Betsy, two goats he kept out in the yard by the shore. He fed them all with fish, so no wonder the place smelt like the sea. He sang to the mermaids at night, and the seals sang back to him.

'It's been empty for ages,' Mum said. 'Once poor Johnny died no one went near the place except the SPCA which came by and cleared all the animals away, and the place is as it was since then. All those sheds and outhouses falling down.'

I bought it with cash from the sale of my shares to Unilever. I thought how Johnny would laugh at the notion of profit from a perfume business buying his fragrant corner. I carved a house sign out of a piece of driftwood from the shore, calling it 'Johnny's.' I cleared out the sheds and outhouses and knocked them down and hired the local joiner to renovate the cottage and moved in as the first frosts of winter arrived. The driftwood from the shore had a sea scent which filled the air all the way through the house.

8

THE HOUSE HAD taken all my perfume money. I saw an advert for a relief postie in the local paper, and applied and got the job, which became permanent a while after. That's how things happen.

It was the best job in the whole world. It gave me an income, but more importantly, a daily knowledge of the island and of all its people. It was like getting to know the periodic table all over again, except that instead of 118 elements the island had a population of 411, when I started, divided into five villages and scattered houses and crofts.

The first thing I did was to prove that I could do the job either wholly on foot or by bicycle. It wasn't that easy, but neither was it impossible. The island is relatively small. Five miles at its longest point and three miles at the widest, and the whole postal circuit is fifteen miles, which I could do walking on a good day or on my bike on a wet and windy day. Folk helped by putting their postal boxes at the road ends, which always saved me several miles walking or cycling every day. And most of the time only half of the people received mail on any given day anyway. Sometimes I kept letters or parcels until it was worth my while delivering them. You get to know what's important and what can wait a day or two.

The island had one hundred and fifty houses, though as the years turned over, more and more became second or holiday homes, and personal handwritten letters almost disappeared. Eventually my postal delivery consisted of dropping brown circulars and advertising leaflets through the letterboxes of empty houses. It was always tempting to bin them, but I did my job and delivered them: who am I to edit or embargo the stuff legally received or read? And latterly even the parcels I used to deliver – those Christmas toys and slices of wedding cake from a granddaughter to her granny – were removed from us and handed over to delivery vans who drove over every day from the mainland across the bonnie bridge.

But at first it was a joy. Walking along by the estate hedgerows with the bag over my shoulders on beautiful spring, summer, and autumn mornings. And especially those crisp winter mornings when you could see your breath rising into the air.

'Morning!'

'Morning!'

'How's things?'

'No bad.'

'Some weather, eh?'

'Beautiful. Absolutely beautiful.'

'Rain tomorrow, though.'

'Aye.'

And there was Mrs Hall watering the roses in her

garden, and young Smith with his head inside the bonnet of a car again, and Nosey Shaw hanging over the gate as usual checking who I was delivering letters or parcels to, and more or less asking me what was in them.

'Another parcel for Jinks, eh? What on earth is he at?'

'After Stamford Bridge, is this my life?' I thought as I trekked through the bog.

Truth was, it was easy enough to know what folk were sending or receiving. And not because I steamed open letters or parcels or scanned them or examined them or looked inside them or anything. As with any other job, you get to know the reality by the appearance. Really without looking at all. The slight feel of the envelope, that little bit of weight or volume that suggested cash or a token, the kind of writing on the cover, the sort of stamp, the envelope or paper that covered the contents. Maybe it's a bit like being a doctor who can gauge a patient's health by the way they enter the room. The message inside is already written on the outside.

My day always started and finished at the bridge. In the morning I collected the mail from the mainland van and left it in the big red box at the end of the day for the same van to take into town. The bridge became the measure for my life. One hundred and fifty yards over and one hundred and fifty yards back. My coming and my going. From island to mainland, from mainland to island. Primroses on this side, foxgloves on the other.

I had my breakfast and tea at the bridge every day

from my haversack. In the morning on this side, while waiting for the mainland van to come over the bridge, in the afternoon on the other, sitting beside the big red box. The water had its eastern and western colours: a tad bluer to the east, a shade more green to the west. A stone one the island side faced east for the morning sun and another on the mainland side faced west for the afternoon, where I sat to have my meal. I took to counting the stones on the bridge as I ate. I reckoned it had about a thousand of them, though it was always impossible to be precise. William Ross later told me the final count: one thousand one hundred and fifty-nine.

As I ate my piece I thought of Olghair MacKenzie. What treasure had he laid there, and where? Spanish doubloons perhaps? And what would they be worth nowadays? I suppose it depends on how many he hid and whether they were real gold and how well they had kept. Though gold always keeps. And then again, where would he have put it? Under which of the thousand stones might the treasure be found? The story itself is the thing, not the treasure.

Treasure Island, then. The Admiral Benbow Inn and Hispaniola, Jim Hawkins, Black Dog, Billy Bones, Captain Flint, Ben Gunn, and the great hero himself, Long John Silver. And the famous map, where X marked the spot. And the Cailleach Bheur who could jump from Mull to Kintyre in three steps. Hop, step, leap. Though MacKenzie's treasure would neither be here nor there. Neither on the island nor on the mainland, but in the no-man's land between the two. How smart of him. I resolved one day to somehow climb the frame of the bridge and mark a spot with an x where Olghair's treasure might be. Best to make it small so that you'd have to be near it to know, for what secret treasure is worth anything when it's visible to all?

Winters were harsh. That constant gale force wind from the north-west and the endless rain. It was tempting these times to use the Post Office van, but a resolution stands. You can't only save the world when it suits you. Neither rain nor wind ever stopped Long John Silver. All I needed were good waterproofs and a way of walking to ease the wind and rain. Mum was forever giving me things to wear to keep extra warm. Gorgeous (if itchy!) woollen socks and ganseys she knitted in that old way of hers, the needles click-clacking by the kitchen range whenever I visited to see how she was.

'You need to keep warm, Jack,' she kept saying. 'Naturally warm, like a sheep. Keeping your body heat in and the cold air out.'

And then she'd make a pot of tea, despite all my offers to make it, knowing that love depends as much on ritual as on alteration. I'd forgotten how uneven earth is. Perhaps I'd become too accustomed to the pavements of London, for here I was stepping into bogs and climbing bits of raggedy paths and avoiding sudden dips and rabbit holes. It was a constant up and down world, pulling me this way and that. I began to think of Dad, for nothing is abstract.

So I learned how to walk best: in the lee of the hill

where you can, and lean forward into the wind, when the natural instinct is to turn sideways. That way it sweeps over you. Most days I felt the wind itself tire of the struggle and ease off after a while. It was as if you could negotiate with nature. If you give it respect and its due, it acknowledges your efforts and relents. I often took the old drove track up the side of the hill, which was a bit of a climb, but was easily the most sheltered way in a storm. The old ruins of make-shift shelters provided some refuge. The same place some Neolithic boy had crouched once upon a time.

I came under a bit of pressure. Mum occasionally moaning that I was 'wasting yourself and your talents. What about your degree in chemistry? Can't you do something with that?', and Mrs Hall always offering me advice.

'You'll catch your death of cold, young man, always walking about in the rain like that. You should get a nice office job like my Billy did. Joined the Civil Service and is now semi-retired on a good pension.'

I was tempted. Not to join the Civil Service, but to set up my own business again. Be independent. Self-sufficient. As if such a thing is possible. And maybe it is. Sitting there, on the hillside on a bright May morning, looking down on to the small green fields and the mostly broken-down stone walls and the blue green sea beyond, as far as the horizon. It startled you sometimes. To trade that in again for what? For buying and selling, no matter how you package it. Organic. Sustainable. You make a thing and market it and sell it, for profit, or at least to cover your costs. Like those card dealers who show you the Queen of Hearts and then put down an Ace. And isn't being a postie or a storyteller the same: taking words and goods from here to there, across watery bridges? The way Mrs MacPherson always looks out for me, waiting for that airmail letter.

No man is an island... not even here. Maybe especially not on The Island, where everyone depends on everyone else for their well-being. As a postie, no job without letters or parcels to deliver. And who else did Mrs Hall and Elsie MacInnes and Nosey Shaw and old Archina Kennedy and Mary MacLaren, who lived on her own out beyond Otter's Point, ever see except the postie? They might have died of boredom and loneliness or a sudden heart attack, unknown and unmissed for ages, if I hadn't been calling by or passing their houses every day. Even a wave of our hands made all the difference to our lives.

Archina was considered a bit of a spey-wife on the island, able to tell the future as well as the past. She was the only one who still used the village well, saying that folk would see the day when they'd sell all they had for a drop of clean water like that.

One Friday morning in September, one of those lovely crisp autumnal mornings, I arrived at Mrs Hall's to deliver her mail. She wasn't out and about as usual, so I went into the porch, which was always open, and there she was lying on her side on the floor in the hallway.

I could see she was still breathing and had just fainted. I propped her up on a cushion and gave her a glass of water to drink and bit by bit she came round, and I asked if she'd like a cup of tea and she asked for a glass of sherry from the cupboard next to the window in the sitting room, and when she sipped that slowly she revived. She even started singing, though that may have been the effect of the sherry.

I led her through to the sitting room where the radio was playing some fiddle music.

'I was sitting there listening to the radio,' she said, 'when my head started throbbing and I felt all hot and flushed and queasy, and that's all I remember until now.'

I stayed with her until she was moving about and starting to make her lunch in the kitchen as if nothing had happened.

'Maybe you should phone the doctor?' I said.

'No. I'll be fine,' she said. 'Old age doesn't come on its own. We stumble on.'

I checked in with her again on the way back and she seemed all right, working away in the garden as usual, checking her raspberry bushes.

Then the following week – again on the Friday morning – I found Elsie MacInnes in the same condition, fainted in her kitchen. She always left her front door open (almost everyone did), and when I called her name there was no answer, so I went in, and found her lying on her side, in almost exactly the same posture as Mrs Hall.

She too revived after I helped her to her chair and gave her some tea and biscuits. She too refused to call the doctor. They were of that generation whose parents remembered having to pay for a doctor's call, so I think they were reluctant to bother.

'I'm fine. I'm fine,' she said. 'Life is never without its little troubles.'

And she too sang the chorus of some old song.

The following week it was Mary MacLaren, and then Shaw and Kennedy. I didn't want to be a tell-tale, for the first rule of being a postie is to be confidential about your customers' affairs. You have to trust. But I was concerned, so I mentioned it to Nurse Morrison, who lived on the mainland side of the bridge.

'I'll drop by and check them all this week,' she said.

'They all seemed fine,' she told me the next time I saw her. 'Blood pressures normal and nothing to be greatly worried about physically. They're all getting on a bit.'

The odd thing was that they'd all five of them lain in the same positions – lying on their right side, right hand outstretched, left hand tucked in over their stomach, and their ankles crossed. It reminded me of something: a game we used to play in primary school called the Giant and the Trolls. While the Giant hid in the playground shelter, all the rest of us would run around the playground for a while. When the Giant roared, we all fell on to the ground in that position, playing dead, and if the Giant saw any of us without our ankles crossed, left hand tucked in over our stomach, right hand outstretched, and lying on our right side, he could gobble us up. Even if we dared as much as breathe while we lay there. And of course someone always did. The only difference with Mrs Hall and Elsie

MacInnes and Nosey Shaw and Archina Kennedy and Mary MacLaren was that as they woke up from their faint they all started singing in Gaelic the moment they came round.

I didn't speak the language. Mostly because I hadn't been born on the island, and in those days it wasn't taught in school either, so if I heard it occasionally, it was only from some old people who had retained it over in the more remote villages. It was sometimes sung at the village hall concerts, but no one of my age or generation ever used it. It was a thing for singing, not speaking.

As I walked up the old drover's road with my mail sack, I paused at MacPherson's Cairn. He was the doctor who had first brought medical services to the area in the nineteenth century, travelling on his packhorse from district to district and staying at inns whenever he could. He continued to travel and visit people all through the great typhus outbreak of the 1890s, and they say that without his aid, thousands would have died. The Island community erected the cairn when he died just after the Great War. It marked the spot where they said he used to come down off his horse and get on his knees to pray before visiting the sick.

You can see the whole island from the cairn. All the little villages and houses scattered like pebbles far below, and the sea stretching west as far as the eye can see, and the high hills of the mainland in the distance on the other side. Here, and there. Directly below is a small, whitewashed cottage in all its plain beauty. So pretty you always want to touch it. It belonged to

Johannes Jansen, a Dutchman. I sat by the cairn, leaning against the inscription on the side. In loving memory of Dr Angus MacPherson, Lighiche, who served this community with distinction. He healeth the broken in heart, and bindeth up their wounds. Psalm 147:3.

It struck me that what had happened to Mrs Hall and Elsie MacInnes and Mary MacLaren and Shaw and Kennedy was that their hearts were broken. They were the only ones on the island who still had a remnant of Gaelic. It connected them all. Only those five would say an occasional 'Madainn mhath' or 'Ciamar a tha thu an-diugh?' to me as a matter of course, even though they knew I could not answer them back. Maybe that's what broke their hearts. That they could say a thing and get no response.

I suppose it was a miniature version of mass hysteria, that outbreak of convulsive dancing in the Middle Ages, and the twitching children in that school in Japan, and the mass fainting in Tanzania. The solidarity of loss and yearning bubbling over like an underground stream.

'Feeling better?' I asked Mrs Hall the following Friday.

'Yes, lad, yes, I am. Thanks for asking. Tapadh leat.'

The two words had slipped out unconsciously, and as they did she shivered, as if she might faint again. But she steadied herself and smiled and said, 'I'd better sit down and have a cup of tea.'

'Will I...?'

'Yes, please,' she said.

She sat in her favourite Parker Knoll chair while I

made the tea. She was singing something.

'Sugar?' I called.

'Two. Though I shouldn't. And the biscuits are in the tin on the middle shelf in the cupboard beside the cooker.'

We sat with our tea and biscuits.

'I wish I'd learned Gaelic,' I said. 'But I didn't get the chance.'

'I wouldn't bother,' she said. 'A dead language. Only a couple of old people like me speak it now.'

I knew that wasn't true, even then.

'Still,' I said. 'It would be nice to have some words. It sounds lovely.'

'Pah! A thing is only lovely if it's useful. Like that fire there – that's lovely because it keeps me nice and warm all through the winter.'

'I'm sure these Gaelic songs you sing do the same too.'

She laughed.

'Except no one understands them,' she said. 'So what's the point?'

'Elsie MacInnes does. And Mary MacLaren. And Shaw and Kennedy. And others would if they could. That's the point.'

'Ha,' she said 'The Famous Five! The Last of the Mohicans!'

'So you talk to each other?'

'Of course. We may live in different villages, but we've got phones, haven't we? And we see each other at church, and sometimes out at the shop or on the bus.

We keep things alive.'

'And when you don't?'

'Well then it gets a bit lonely. And the phones were down lately too, as you know. So then we talk to old friends. That's how it is.'

'What's your favourite song?' I asked.

'"Ballachullish Glen",' she said, without hesitation. 'Though that's not what it's called. It's called "Gleann Bhaile Chaoil".'

'Will you sing it to me?'

'I don't have a voice.'

'Of course you do, Mrs Hall. I've heard you.'

She sang, and it was like watching something fragile and brittle being moved by unsteady hands. The same way she moved when carrying the china teapot and cups and saucers and milk and biscuits on the tin tray. I wanted to reach out and steady things, but of course I couldn't. I didn't have the language to do it. I hummed along quietly as best I could, leaving her to tread her way through the shaky verses.

'It's what brought the fit on,' she said, once she'd finished, and composed herself. 'Elsie and Mary and Shaw and Kennedy said the same thing. You see, we were at school together, and we always sang that song. And then we all stopped singing it, and that day, weeks ago, when you found me and then all of them on the floor, it was because we heard ourselves on the radio. A programme the BBC recorded years and years ago when we were little children. I heard it first and then told the others and one by one they listened to the repeats, and that's how you found us. Once the broadcasts stopped, we all got better.'

Mrs Hall took a sip of tea. 'I suppose our illness was about everything we lost. At times it feels as if the five of us live on another island in another world, far, far away. We were all children playing down on the shore last week, and now here we are.' She smiled. 'We used to play this great game, the Giant and the Trolls. We all took turns at being the Giant trying to catch someone in the wrong position or breathing when they should have been dead still.'

She'd been talking as if to herself, but then looked straight at me. 'O, and by the way,' she added. 'I was a nurse too once upon a time, so I suspected the same as you. I learned all about trauma and hysteria in my days at Craig Dunain. They said you needed to make a thing strange to yourself to cope.'

How little we know about each other.

9

UNEXPECTEDLY, ONE DAY, Charlotte arrived at the door.
All those other memories in an instant. London. Austria.
The going of ways.

'Hi,' she said. 'Just thought I'd drop by.'

She looked wonderful. Happy. Tanned.

'You look great,' I said.

'You too. You too. What's doing?'

'Oh, this and that. Postman Pat!'

'I heard.'

'Oh?'

'I got the bus to the bridge. Local man sitting next to
me. I asked him about you.'

'And what did he say?'

'"O! Jack the Postman. Used to be a football player,"
he said.'

'And you?'

'Oh, this and that. Health and wealth. Well, the
health bit anyway.'

'Glad to hear it. Are you...?'

'Passing through. Unless you're offering accom-
modation.'

'You know me. Fàilt' is furan.'

'Meaning?'

'Welcome and make yourself at home.'

'Tea?' she asked, making her way toward the kitchen.

'As long as it's not herbal.'

'What d'you have?'

I watched her rummaging through the shelves.

'Tetley. Yuck. Earl Grey, Lady Grey, Yorkshire. How about that? Yorkshire it is then. A proper brew.'

We seemed more relaxed with each other than we'd ever been. Because we had nothing to gain or lose, or because we were older. And sober.

'How about a walk?'

'Perfect,' she said.

'Long or short?'

'Medium.'

'Okay. We'll go to the loch.'

The road took us through the small birch wood down to Loch na h-Eala, the Loch of the Swan. They say the swan was Jessie MacEacharn, who grieved so much over the loss of her lover in the Jacobite uprising that she turned into a swan.

'So,' she said, when we sat down at the edge of the loch, 'how are things really going?'

'Things are going… magnificently,' I said.

'That's a big word.'

'Not that big. But true. I live simply.'

'It's such a long time since I've smelt lichen and moss and wild garlic,' she said.

'You're not going to tempt me, Charley. That's all behind me.'

It was one of the things she changed when she stopped drinking. 'My childhood pet name,' she'd told me. 'Charley. It makes me… happy! Secure.'

'I've discarded a lot, Jack. Except for my own bath. And potions. They were mad days though, eh?'

'Thought we were it.'

'No one's ever it. Except in the school playground.'

'Not even there.'

I don't know. You do so many things and don't fully know why. Instinct, I suppose, or sympathy or memory or desire or something. But I put my hand over hers and she turned hers to clasp mine.

'I'm sorry I made such a mess of things,' she said. 'All that stuff. I can hardly believe it was me.'

'Me too.'

We stopped by Shiela's Seafood Shack on the way back and bought some fresh crab and lobster. Shiela added in some free prawns. We had great fun cooking it. The large pot on the stove, boiling water, butter, a couple of lemon wedges, garlic cloves, dill, thyme, parsley, bay leaves, a few onions, and when the broth was all set in with the crab legs, crab claws, and lobster tails, we added the prawns at the very end. Served with bread. From the oven.

'And you?'

'All good,' she said. 'Keeping myself and all my – clients – healthy.'

'I suppose you could do that anywhere?'

'Like here, for example?'

'Like here, for example.'

'Except I don't want to. I mean, run that business from here. It seems… it seems… wrong.'

'Wrong?'

'Well, I'm not sure that's the right word. But it doesn't feel… right. Because it doesn't. It's because… it's because it feels like bringing something in rather than something which has happened. Organically, as it were.'

'Ha! Everything happens that way, Charley. I came here. Went away. Then came back. Nothing much organic about that.'

'But you *belong*. You've been here since you were a child. You know the place and the people organically, if you want to put it that way.'

'Sort of. But I'm still as much a stranger here as I ever was.'

'Really? I don't believe you.'

And she was right. It was that night in the graveyard that made me truly belong to the place. The strange solidity – the seeming eternity – of the stones compared to the way they shone in the moonlight, with the names so clear and solid. Even the ones that had faded or were overgrown with moss were still and certain, as if all doubt had gone. Here we are, they said. Take us or leave us, good and bad, fragile as we were in our time, like ice, or solid as might have appeared, like rock. And it was Sally, whom I should have loved better. When the opportunity was there to have said those three infinite words to her so that we could have embraced and kissed and held tight forever and ever, even running across the seawall and over the strand and all the way through

Mrs Nicolson's hedge-maze garden and across the moor and over the mountains and crags until we became one with the sickle moon and stars, setting us free from time and place, from the fear of the dark and the unspoken and the unsaid, the errors and mistakes and regrets that haunted me. I had cheated myself of love. Didn't take the chance. To love was everything, and here we were again – this time Charley and me, if she was willing. We were no strangers.

'So much baggage…' she said.

'That too can go. Fling it into the river. Or into the air. Or into the ground. It can take it. It's all biodegradable.'

'Dust to dust, ashes to ashes?'

'No. Much more than that. To grow again. Out of the embers.'

'Why don't we,' she said, 'cook the rest of the prawns on the open fire? You know, as in proper, rather than controlled cooking?' And we did, setting them in tinfoil over the wood to crackle and sparkle as the prawn juices seeped through. We talked nice and easy, the way you talk when an open fire is going and the daylight begins to fade.

'I'm glad we left London,' she said. 'It was the beginning of a thing. Which is never enough unless you complete it. I've always… I've always,' she said, 'wanted to be a fisherman. Is that the right word, or should it be fisherwoman? Or fisherperson?'

'Fisher? Iasgair.'

'Iasgair. That's nice. So, maybe I could stay here and fish. Be an iasgair?'

'I've no doubt you could. Have you ever... have you ever fished before?'

'I caught a sprat once, rock-fishing with Grampa in Wales.'

'As in Jack Sprat could eat no fat?'

'We caught a dozen of them and Grampa fried them over a fire of sticks on the shore. It was the best food I've ever tasted.'

'MacLean's got a boat,' I said. 'I'm sure he'd take you on. He's always looking for someone to help him with the creels. We'll go see him tomorrow.'

'Can you swim?' MacLean asked.

'Well enough,' Charlotte said.

'Maybe that's too well. It's not good for a fisherman to be able to swim. If you're going to drown you're better drowning quickly.'

She wasn't sure if he was joking. He wasn't. Still went by the old fable that the less you knew about things the better.

'But that's fine,' he said. 'I'll be sailing tomorrow morning. Leaving from here at seven. Have you got oilskins and boots or anything? No? Doesn't matter – I've plenty.'

And that's how Charlotte became an iasgair. She took to it, if you'll pardon the expression, like a duck to water. Mostly they were day trips, out at seven in the morning to haul in the creels from the night before, and back around five, laying them all back in rows near the skerries and reefs on the eastern side of the waters. But sometimes they were away from seven in the morning till midnight, creeling way beyond Sgeir nan Sgarbh and An Dubh Sgeir down towards Islay.

'That kind of long day is worth a week in itself,' MacLean said.

As it happened, he was nearing retiring stage, and was planning to move down to Ayrshire to be nearer his married daughter and grandchildren. He offered Charlotte the best deal imaginable if she could raise enough money to buy the boat.

'I will throw in the creels and gear for free,' he added. 'Oh, and this camera. It's part of the boat. Just an old Pentax, but it takes good pictures. You'll get tired of taking photographs of seals, but it's worth having it for the occasional shark.'

So it was back to the bank for Charley, now with no Davidson to advise her. She secured a loan on the back of her CV and became – we think – the first full-time female iasgair skipper on the west coast of Scotland.

'But only if you exclude Maebh of the Thousand Ships and Sgàthach and Crooked Annie the Pirate,' MacLean said. 'They caught more fish – and men – than Captain Ahab himself.'

The fishing went well. We had no need to ever buy lobsters or crabs or prawns from the seafood shack again, and Charley could supply them to Shiela and all the other hotels and shops in the area. But it was the sea itself she loved. The way it led you, so that you never mastered or controlled it, but followed its ways and patterns. You learned daily how fragile you were. I never liked it so much, though I was on it often enough, crewing for Charley on my days off from the postal delivery and then again when she decided to do some night fishing and we'd sail out west as the light began to fade, guided by her growing knowledge of the waters and seas all around.

Night fishing was more fun. Those things that were big and clear during the day became small and obscure in the night. And sometimes the other way round: skerries and reefs you couldn't see under the sun glittered sharply in the moonlight. But mostly it was the sound of the night we loved. The soft throb of the engine carrying over the still waters, the faraway sounds that carry in the darkness – a dog barking at some farmhouse, a motorcycle revving, a person calling or crying. Once, in the twilight, as we sailed between Eilean a' Chladaich and Glas Eilean, we heard the sound of psalm singing, the precentor laying out the line as clear as a bell and the congregation joining in like the soft swell of the sea. Maybe it was from far off Iona. We never knew.

The thing that struck me when out fishing was how thin the land looked. When I walked the drover's road, the slope fell away to my left and the heathery hill above rose to the heights. But from sea it all looked so – I'm not sure of the word, but perhaps insignificant. Less solid, as it were. I'd noticed the folk who lived in the glens spoke more quietly, as if they were content with their lot, like sheep, while those who lived next to the sea were louder, as if afraid they wouldn't be heard because of the waves.

It reminded me of myself when I first came to the island: uncertain of whether to say something or be quiet. To balance sound and silence. In contrast, the sea was all voice. Whether on the rare quiet days, murmuring away, or when the wind whipped it into a white froth and our boat rocked up and down, trusting in the wisdom of the waves. To believe, despite what we were seeing.

'Listen,' Charley said.

The swell rose and fell in with a deep, heavy sound.

'It's when it cries with a thin sort of whine you worry,' she said. 'At the moment, it's like a big teddy bear rumbling away. We'll be fine. Always listen to its song, Jack, rather than look at its face.'

And she was smiling, surprised too with her knowledge.

10

I SUPPOSE WE all took the bridge for granted. It had always been there, had it not? You walked or cycled or drove over it and you were on the mainland, or if coming from the mainland, on the island. The road – the gap – between here and there.

Sometimes in winter Charley and I drove over it to the nearest town where the cinema was. We saw *Star Wars* and *Saturday Night Fever* and *Edward Scissorhands*. And we always had that feeling you have when you leave the cinema, like you are entering a different, black and white world. The town itself was as sad as sin in the winter dark. The yellow lights of the few hotels, the orange streetlights flickering in the puddles, the wind blowing things about the pier. A couple or two hurrying through the rain with their bags of chips. It made us feel old when we went there. Maybe towns need to be cities, like London, to work? Otherwise they're nothing. Neither here nor there, but middle-aged, where everything and nothing is news. Not just what Flora said down at the Post Office this morning but everything that pours at us from the four corners of the earth.

Alex MacLean the creel fisherman always said the earth had eight corners: north, north-east, east, south-east, south, south-west, west, north-west. Except he pronounced them nor, nor-east, and so on.

'That's where Big Archie blows from,' he said. 'He travels round the world on a horse and stops now and again to rest his horse and blow his horn. When the wind blows on a clear night you can see his puffed-out cheeks as frothy clouds in the sky.' It made no difference when we argued that a round globe could have no corners.

'It's just a word,' he said. 'Like a bridge is a bridge, whether here or in Sydney.'

But it was clear to everyone that we lived in this corner of the universe, while they – the mainlanders – lived in that corner. In that vast expanse that went on and on and on. As MacLean put it, folk were blowing their horns in Oban same as in Edinburgh or London or Paris or New York or wherever. What a noise!

Not that they were better or worse than us. Just not us. And who was I to talk? The nervous little boy who came here all those years ago, desperate to fit in and finding myself not quite in the centre, not shunned, neither here nor there. Forever crossing the bridge, as it were, hoping for an easy rest on either or both sides.

It was the day the school bus broke down on the way home, stuck in the snow. Some of the parents came in Land Rovers and in cars with chains on their tyres to take their children home, but Sally said to me, 'Let's walk back,' and we were the only ones who did.

When we reached the bridge she reached over and put her hand in mine. Not like when we were wee and we'd skip across by the seawall, but different. Our hands were bigger, and we were teenagers, and hers felt ever so cold, so I caressed it, hoping she'd think it was because I was trying to warm it but knowing fine that we both knew it was because I loved her and wanted to hold her hand like that forever on a bridge that never reached the other side. She let go as soon as we reached the island.

'We were safe together,' she said, and we then ran through the falling snow all the way home.

The news about the bridge first appeared in the local paper. The council engineers found a dangerous fault line. It needed to close for further inspections. A temporary ferry would run instead, but for passengers only, because neither side of the water had adequate piers to handle a car ferry.

'Just like the good old days,' some said, while others complained, 'What happens in an emergency?' 'How will an ambulance get over?' 'How will I get my shopping?' 'What if I need to go to Glasgow?'

But the passenger ferry worked fine. Folk drove up to one side and parked and then did that remarkable thing of walking from their cars to the ferry and then walked on to the bus or to a friend's car waiting on the other side. As if, given any inconvenience or chaos, given Armageddon itself, people could adapt and cope.

The crack in the bridge was even worse than the

engineers first suspected. The huge increase in traffic over the years, especially articulated lorries, buses, motorhomes, and heavy equipment, were putting too much stress on a stone bridge that had been designed for a horse and cart, or – at best – the occasional Morris Traveller bringing some tourists over to see the waterfall at Beinn an Dròbha. As if that was a surprise. The first engineers said the old bridge was simply irreparable. It would need to be replaced by something much stronger and safer.

'Not that it will affect me anyway, since I'll soon be off to another corner of the world, but I hate to see something so beautiful destroyed for lack of care,' said MacLean. 'All our memories are tied up with crossing this old bridge, and all they need is a team of stonemasons to dismantle it stone by stone. These modern engineers can install a steel span inside it all the way across, then cover it with all the old stones. And there's Baile Dubh quarry for any gaps. If they did the work like that the bridge would look exactly as it did when it was built four hundred years ago. I'm sure Archimedes would approve,' he added, as if that somehow sealed the deal.

The desire of older folk like Alex MacLean to keep things as they were. For things to look as they always did. Make time stand still. The council and the central government officials who had to find the money to pay for the new bridge suggested a straight flat bridge, which would look much more modern, and also come in at a third of the price of an arched one.

'But what about boats?' we said, and they suggested a flat swing bridge – the kind you see on canals – which would occasionally open to let boats sail through, but that too was rejected at a public meeting. Eventually, MacLean's suggestion was agreed to, and the process of dismantling the bridge stone by stone began. The contract went to the local stonemason, William Ross.

He took his time. He was in no great hurry to see all that traffic back on the road. As a craftsman with a small team of workers, he made sure each stone was carefully marked so that it would go back exactly where it had been. William Ross came to know each stone. Its shape and texture, dimension and place, the same as, once upon a time, I knew the entire periodic table off by heart, each element like a stone in the wall, from H for Hydrogen at the top left to Og for Oganesson at the bottom right.

Though, like bridges, the table is malleable into all kinds of different shapes and sizes, from an arch to a circle to something new as discoveries are made. Nothing is fixed.

William Ross found Olghair MacKenzie's buried treasure. It was a small brass box hidden behind stone number 759, which lay at the top right-hand side of the arch of the bridge. Maybe around the place where O for Oxygen sits in the periodic table. Inside the box was a hand-written scroll.

'It must be Gaelic,' he said to himself.

He couldn't speak or read the language, but knew

enough to recognise it. Like how even if you're not a fisherman, you sort of recognise the difference between a herring and a mackerel. He recognised the word 'gealach' ('moon') and thought 'Spàinnteach' must have something to do with Spain – or maybe spoons – and the scroll was signed at the bottom 'Olghair MacCoinnich witness confirmatio'. Olghair MacKenzie. And that nightmare year in high school when he had for some mad reason chosen to do Latin came flooding back to him: confirming witness. Was MacKenzie a witness to someone else?

Now, William Ross had been in school with me, and although I was no great friends with him, we knew each other. He knew I had been the headmaster's son and had an interest in Gaelic. He knew that Archina Kennedy and Mary MacLaren and a couple of other older folk could speak the language, though reading and writing and using it had been purged out of schools in their day. I wasn't any better at understanding it than he was, but I could read a little, so I told him I'd read it to one of the native speakers next time I was over with the post.

'This is an older form of Gaelic,' Archina said. 'And this is what it means: "To the finder of this document I bear witness that not a league from here when the eighth-by-eight moon shines over the peak of Rubh' na h-Achlais, the Òr Spàinnteach can be found in the hollow of the cliff. Olghair MacCoinnich, witness confirmatio."'

'Meaning?'

'That us children and old people were right all along.'

'Òr Spàinnteach means Spanish Gold?'

'Aye.'

'And a league?'

'About three and a half miles. My Grampa used to say it was the distance a person could walk in an hour. He was a sailor, and when he got tipsy he used to sing.' And she sang:

Farewell and adieu to you, Spanish ladies,
Farewell and adieu to you, ladies of Spain;
For we've received orders for the sail of old England,
But we hope very soon we shall see you again.
We'll rant and we'll roar like true British sailors,
We'll rant and we'll roar all on the salt seas;
Until we strike soundings in the channel of old England:
From Ushant to Scilly it's thirty-five league.

'That's all I know about leagues,' she said. 'O, and my grandfather's name was Olghair. It's Norse.'

William Ross visited Charley and me that evening. We looked at the scroll together.

'Of course she's right,' Charlotte said. 'A league is about three-and-a-bit miles. Four-point-three kilometres.'

'Rubh' na h-Achlais? Do you know, William?'

'No. No idea. Never heard of it.' And because these were the days before mobile phones and search engines, we fetched out the Ordnance Survey map of the area, and didn't find it.

'And the eighth-by-eight moon?'

'Maybe he meant the eighth planet? Which one is that again?'

'Neptune. But he'd never mistake the moon for a planet.'

'Maybe the eighth phase of the moon,' said Charlotte. 'I studied them in the navigation chart. Let me find it.'

It was in the drawer. She read.

'The moon goes through eight phases every month. The new moon, waxing crescent, first quarter, waxing gibbous, full moon, waning gibbous, third quarter, and waning crescent. So that's the eighth moon of the month. It looks like a thin crescent of light to the left. The one the local people here call the sickle moon. Ideal for harvesting the corn.'

'How long does that last?' asked Ross.

'Around six days. Maybe seven. Depending,' she said.

'If we ever find it,' William Ross said before he left, 'it's fifty-fifty. Okay?'

'You mean we're twenty-five per cent each and you're fifty,' I said.

'Aye, 's fair enough, isn't it? Finders Keepers and all that, but I'll give you the half if you find it with me.'

We shook hands on it and had prawn sandwiches to celebrate.

11

WHILE WILLIAM ROSS and his team were dismantling
the old bridge, discussions continued about the new
one. All were agreed that the facing – 'the aesthetic'
as the chief planning officer put it – should be as
before, but there were other proposals too. Johannes
Jansen argued that a tidal energy system should be
incorporated into the new design.

These were very early days for that kind of
development here, but Jansen said the technology was
already widely in use in Holland. 'It's the future,' he
stated, 'based on the simple technology of the past.' So
he was asked to do a special presentation to the bridge
engineers and government officials and the community
in the village hall.

He flipped charts and showed slides and sketches
and drawings. Rather than putting the turbines below
water, which he argued was too shallow anyway, he
proposed paddle wheels which would turn on the side
of the bridge to harness energy. Even better, he argued,
would be for the paddle wheels to hang vertically from
the span of the bridge, so they would also gain wind
traction.

'Not only that,' he said, 'but they will look remarkable and be guaranteed to attract thousands of visitors to the area to see them. A little bit of Holland in Scotland, as it were. And, they will be aesthetically pleasing,' he added, to impress the planning officer. He spoke as if it could all come true.

We all loved the designs and drawings he showed. Pencil spirals here, there, and everywhere, with ladders and spires and spikes and chutes where the water flowed.

'That was a bit Heath Robinson!'

'More Breughel,' he said.

Johannes's proposals were, of course, turned down. Though now, as the world burns, everyone regrets we didn't take his advice.

'Crazy,' some said.

'Would never work.'

'Far too expensive.'

'It's a road bridge we need, not a work of art.'

As if the stone bridge was not itself a work of art in the first place.

So the steel people arrived from Germany once William and his gang had removed all the original stones, and the steel arches were put in place. All the stones, including Olghair MacKenzie's with the brass box (but minus the scroll), were put back where they'd been, and it seemed as if the bridge was as before. Except stronger and safer and without its secret clue.

'Any progress with Rubh' na h-Achlais?' I said to William Ross any time I saw him on my round, and he'd shake his head.

'No,' he said, 'but I've been walking a league in every direction from the bridge to try and find it.'

'"Not a league" is what the document said.'

'So, it's not a league?'

'I dunno. Maybe he meant just short of a league. Or maybe he meant it's not a league at all. Maybe he meant no league or two leagues or a dozen leagues? It's like saying not a chance, isn't it? Which means no chance. So maybe he meant no league? Maybe he meant it was where he left the note, in or at or near the bridge itself?'

'I'm not dismantling that bridge again,' he said. 'Not for all the gold in China.'

'Or Spain.'

Mary MacLaren lived in the last house in Rubha Garbh. She kept a good herd of cows and provided milk to one of the big dairies on the mainland who came over twice a week to collect from her. Their customers all said that Mary MacLaren's cows provided the best milk for cheese-making in the whole country.

'It's all to do with rotation,' she said. 'Where the horses are this year the tatties grow there the next, and where the pigs root this year becomes pastures green for the cows next.'

She was always the last person on my delivery round, though I rarely had to go there, because she hardly ever received any mail. Sometimes I went over to see her anyway to see how she was – and to hear her beautiful Gaelic and practice my own! When I called, she always asked me in for a cup of tea, and since it was the last stop on my round anyway I always said yes. She made the best ginger biscuits that could float like a ship in her strong tea.

That day I had a small parcel for her. After I handed it over, she said, 'Come in.'

I always sat in the kitchen, where she spent most of her time pottering about.

When we spoke Gaelic, she did her best with me and was patient, which I know is not easy when you're trying to explain something and the other person only understands a percentage of what you're saying. But maybe that's how it is anyway, even when you're fluent in any language. Who really knows what anyone is saying, or trying to say?

'Ciamar a tha thu an-diugh?' she asked, and I gave the stock answer, 'Tha gu math, tapadh leibh.' I'm well, thank you. Like spending someone else's money. And that 'leibh' (instead of 'leat') is the respectful plural of 'you', as in the French 'tu' and 'vous'. We talked back and forth for a while about the weather and she asked me whether the path was wet or dry today and I said 'tioram' (dry) and she asked if it was 'caran tioram' (quite dry) or 'anabarrach tioram' (very dry) and I said it was uamhasach tioram.

She was always more concerned with the way I said a word rather than the meaning of the word. The 'blas' (taste) of the language, as she put it. For I could have all the words in the world, but if I didn't have a good 'blas' it was like a cow without good creamy milk.

'Am fac' thu a' ghealach an-raoir?' ('Did you see the

moon last night?') she asked, and I said I did and she said it was called 'Gealach buidhe an abachaidh' (The yellow moon of the harvest). And she talked for a while about how in the old days of her youth they used to cut the corn by sickle even under the light of the moon, such was the hurry – the need – to get it in before the weather broke.

'You always sow under a waxing moon and reap under the waning one,' she said.

And then I asked her, 'Do you know what the eighth-by-eight moon is?'

She seemed surprised that I used the phrase.

'The eighth-by-eight moon? Why, the eighth moon phase of the eighth month.'

'Of August?'

'Not necessarily.'

And she explained how, in the old days of her youth, the Gaelic months were counted differently. Counted in quarters, so that the year began with 'Ciad Mìos an Earraich' ('The First Month of Spring'), and so forth through 'Mìos deireannach a' Gheamhraidh' ('The Last Month of Winter').

'But the thing is, Jack, that in those days they didn't use January, February, March and so on, and that "first month of spring" was likely equivalent to our February. So spring fell around our February, March, and April. Then summer would be May, June, and July. Autumn – August, September, and October, and winter, November, December, and January. The moon of the eight month would be in our Sultain – September. Or maybe at the end of August or in early October, depending on where the moon cycle was at the beginning of February. Everything always depends on everything else.'

'And did you ever hear anything about Olghair MacCoinnich? I know there were stories about him, but did you ever hear anything specific? Who he was or anything like that?'

'How long have you got?' she asked.

'Cho fad sa dh'fheumas – as long as it takes, Mrs MacLaren.'

'Well. They say he was the illegitimate son of the Bishop of Perth and Mairianna MacKenzie, Dowager of Lord Pithaven, who died on the scaffold, accused of adultery with a prelate, driven by witchcraft. Olghair went to the University of St Andrews and was ordained, but then went overseas, first to France and Spain and Italy and then on to Palestine where it seems he trained as a doctor and worked for a while in Cairo and Alexandria. It was there that he learned all about magic, they say, and one of the stories is that he could transport himself anywhere he named by chanting the name of the place he was going to a thousand times. But his greatest claim to fame was that he finally discovered the secret of alchemy and of turning stone or iron or brass or anything like that into pure gold. The Egyptians claimed he stole these secrets from them, so he fled for his life and returned to Scotland and ended up here as an itinerant friar and healer, moving from place to place and earning his bread by whatever work came along, whether it was preaching or leeching blood from the sick or rowing boats across waters or erecting stone buildings or whatever was needed. They say he brought back some Spanish gold and others say he didn't bring anything except the rags he was wearing but had the power to turn stone into gold and that the two stories somehow got mixed up.'

She dunked her digestive biscuit into her tea. 'That's how I heard it anyway.'

Mrs MacLaren then solved the third part of the puzzle.

'Do you know where Rubh' na h-Achlais is?'

'Rubh' na h-Achlais? Well, Rubh', as you probably know by now, means Ridge or Point. The proper word is Rubha, but people shorten it when they speak and tend to leave that last vowel out and say Rubh'. Achlais is armpit or oxter. So, The Ridge of the Armpit. It's the one over on the north-east there, shaped like your armpit when you drink a cup of tea. Of course, they don't call it that now. I think the Ordnance Survey people gave it the name Oxter Ridge which folk nowadays call Ox Ridge, which has got nothing to do with any ox or beast.'

12

IT TOOK US five years to find the spot. We knew where Ox Ridge was – a rocky V-shaped ridge running towards the western sea cliff edge. It was pretty devoid of grass or any kind of vegetation, so the name Ox Ridge had been a bit of a puzzle to people.

'Maybe it was more fertile in the old days,' some said.

'Or that oxen don't need much grass.'

'What happened,' Mary MacLaren said, 'was that the locals made a joke and the joke stuck. For at one time the great Oxbridge scholar and climber Professor Armstrong used to come here and climb the cliffs and folk made fun of him. Wandering about in his plus-fours and big boots with a tent and coils of ropes and iron nails and compasses and maps. Always carried a bag of doughnuts with him. Claimed they gave him energy. Not many people went over there, so they nicknamed it Oxbridge for a laugh and it stuck, with the next generation thinking it was 'ridge'. Which of course it is.'

Our challenge was not to find Oxridge (or its etymology) but the exact spot indicated by Olghair MacKenzie. To the finder of this document I bear witness that not a league from here when the eighth-by-eight moon shines over the peak of Rubh' na h-Achlais, the Òr Spàinnteach can be found in the hollow of the cliff. Olghair MacCoinnich, witness confirmatio.

We measured a league from the bridge to Rubha na h-Achlais, which had two peaks, and the hollow in between like the bent elbow between the hand and shoulder holding Mrs MacLaren's cup of tea. The eighth-by-eight moon was the biggest challenge. We studied the moon charts, and that first year the moon was in its eighth stage between the fifth and twelfth of September.

We took turns, William on one night and Charley and I on the next, to bivvy there overnight in the hope of catching a beam of moonlight or something that would give us a clue. Unfortunately, that first year was all cloudy and overcast, and we hardly saw any moon except for one clear night when it shone in all its glory. That night you could believe that MacKenzie's treasure was everywhere, with the sea and rivers and lochs and streams and moor and rocks and all the houses far below and the million stars far above all shining like gold.

The second year was also all cloudy and dark. The third better, because the waning crescent moon was visible every night. However, mist hovered over the island and even when the moon shone we couldn't see where the light landed.

The fourth year gave us hope. One night, as the light was emerging over the mainland to the east, the top curve of the sickle moon seemed to glitter for a moment on a low piece of ground at the bottom of the cliff, but when we searched there at first light, we found only remnants of the wings of a single-seater plane from the war. At least we were able to report it to the local war museum, which then rescued part of the aircraft registration tail number and gave it to the family of the descendants of the pilot.

Isn't it strange how obsessive a thing becomes? I think William Ross was different, in the sense that he was genuinely interested in the gold – in the money – while I became obsessed with the search itself. Working out the puzzle, as in find-the-cat or solitaire or chess. Maybe like my football days when the ball was on the wing and I had to judge where to run so as to meet it at exactly the right moment, before the defender got there. Or more like my days as a chemist, I thought, as I lay there in my bag in the moonlight wondering, if 1.00 mol of a gas occupies 24.0 dm^3 at room temperature and pressure, what would be the volume of carbon dioxide that could be produced from 0.644 mmol of benzene?

And then in that fifth year of the watch, at the time of the eighth moon phase, we found it. Charley and I were on duty that night, and the sickle moon was shining in all her beauty. It was a cloudless, starry night, the vastness of the universe on display, and our own little corner in it – our wee island – was so small. As we lay there, admiring the glory of the sky, a shooting star rose out from the top edge of the moon and fell in a slow silver arc towards us, coming to rest on the peak of Rubh' na h-Achlais before falling and hovering three quarters of the way up the cliff edge. It then vanished in a shower of light over towards the bridge and beyond, out to sea.

Enough light filtered down from the moon and stars for us to focus our binoculars on the cliff edge where the meteor had paused. Charley took a bearing from the compass and marked it down. Next morning the three of us made for the spot. The cliff edge was too steep to ascend, but William said the way to access the hollow was to walk the ridge and then descend by rope. Something he was used to in his work. His ropes, harness, belay device, and helmet were in his work van anyway at the path end of the ridge, and once we fetched these, we lowered him down the cliff edge.

Some of the autumn geese had already arrived and were settling in on Loch na h-Eala. We could hear their happy voices carrying across the moor and upwards in the still of the late September morning.

Then William called from below,

'There's a ledge. Walk to the other end of the ridge. There's a narrow ledge you can walk along to where I am.'

His voice echoed across the silence. We wondered whether anyone down in the villages would hear him call. The geese did, for they went silent as he spoke, then resumed their own conversations as soon as he was quiet. Charley and I walked to the end of the ridge and saw the small ledge.

'I'd rather go down on the rope,' I said, but she encouraged me.

'It'll be fine. I'll go first.'

We walked slowly along the ledge, leaning towards the cliff. I remembered once reading Blondin's advice after crossing Niagara Falls.

'The secret is never to look down.'

So we didn't, and we arrived safely where William stood. It was more of a cave than a hollow. William had his torch bound round his head, shone it into a corner of the cave and said, 'See. There it is.'

Something shone in the darkness.

'A gold ingot,' William said. 'I went over and looked.'

And then, as if he were a wee boy, added,

'But I didn't touch it.'

The taboos that haunt us! Those things we read in childhood or overheard on the school bus or the playground or we saw at the pictures or were told by folk we admired or revered or feared all those years ago. If you stand on that line you'll turn into a pig. If you eat that, your teeth will fall out. If you don't give me money I'll break your leg. If you miss this penalty, you'll get a fortune. Wicked old man, are you hungry today? If you are, then we will all run away. And then they'd all leave you standing there on your own in the corner of the field.

We all thought of the curse of Tutankhamun. The curse that always followed the finding of a stolen treasure. We might die instantly. Or slowly. Everything we touch becoming gold so that we could never again eat a grape or smell a rose or wash our feet in the sea. But surely there was no curse here? Only that statement of fact from Olghair MacKenzie: I bear witness that not a league from here when the eighth-by-eight moon shines over the peak of Rubh' na h-Achlais, the Òr Spàinnteach can be found in the hollow of the cliff. Olghair MacCoinnich, witness confirmatio. No warnings or threats there. And is a shooting star not a sign of blessing?

We used to play 'Bogey' at school when it got dark early in the winter. The child who was to be the bogey went and hid in some dark place (behind the coal cellar usually), and while he or she was away hiding we'd all stand in a circle in the middle of the playground singing out loud, 'Tonight's the night, a very dark night, Let's hope there'll be no ghosts tonight,' and we'd chant that as we searched and then all of a sudden the bogeyman would jump out and scare us and we'd all go screaming after each other and the first one who was caught in the chase became the next bogeyman. Was he there, over in the dark, crouching at the back of the cave?

Nevertheless. Nevertheless, we all hesitated. That was just a game.

'Something's written on it,' William said. 'I couldn't make out what.'

We walked over to the gold block, led by William's torch. We stood over it, looking down, then got on our knees beside it, still not touching the gold. You never know. It was about the size of a primary school jotter. Maybe six inches wide and six inches long. Something like that. None of us knew what the writing was. It had strokes and signs and symbols, the sort we'd all seen in hieroglyphs or maybe in Chinese or Arabic scripts:

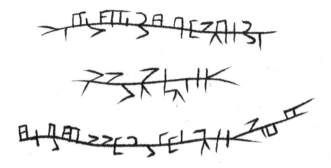

'It's not old Gaelic?' William asked. 'Or Ogham, or something like that?'

'Tell you what,' Charley said. 'Why don't I come back tomorrow with my camera and take a photograph. Then we can research what the writing means. That's the first step. The gold will be safest here. After all, it's been here for centuries untouched. It's not going to vanish overnight.'

We agreed, and the day after Charley and I returned with the camera to take the photograph. I shone the torch on the tablet while Charley clicked away. The sound echoed round the stone walls. It felt as if the cave itself was taking the photographs, not us.

13

WHEN THE FILM was developed it showed nothing but a cloudy haze where the ingot and writing should have been, as if the developer has smudged the film in the lab. He was adamant he didn't.

'It was ever so odd. The image was showing on the negative but vanished when developed.'

And he showed us. There it was: the image clear as day. When he put it into the developing fluid, it disappeared. We returned to the cave and tried again. And again, and every time the same thing happened.

'Tell you what,' William said. 'I'm forever carving names onto stones. The best way to replicate an inscription is to do a rubbing. With this.'

He showed us a plain piece of red carbon paper. So we went once more and William did the rubbing, and sure enough the inscription was copied.

Nowadays we'd be able to scan the image and search it online, but these were the pre-internet days, so Charley said our best bet was to contact one of the universities to see if some historian or linguist could decipher it for us.

'Oxford or Cambridge,' I suggested. 'After all, it

came from Oxridge!'

We phoned Oxford and asked to speak to someone in the Classical Archaeology or Linguistics department and they shuttled us from scholar to scholar who said that deciphering an ancient – or was it medieval, they asked? – scroll was not their forte, and they would pass us on to another professor who suggested another and then another.

We finally ended up speaking to Professor Yosomato from the Faculty of Linguistics, Philology and Phonetics. He couldn't make heads or tails of it, though he suggested it was, most likely, a unique combination of differing demotic signs and symbols, caused either by slovenly writing or – much more likely, he said – an attempt by the inscriber to confuse any possible reader.

We hadn't told him where the actual inscription had come from, though he voluntarily added, 'Perhaps it's art? To be enjoyed, not understood? Or translated – or maybe mistranslated? But I suppose that's how life is anyway: a confusion over what anything means. It's what keeps me in work.'

In my days as a chemist, exactitude was all that mattered. Or at least all I aspired to. What was the use of a formula that was wrong, a prescription that was inaccurate, a calculation that was incomprehensible? A salve could just as easily be a poison by misjudging the ingredients or mistaking the measures. Never confuse 5mg for 5mcg. Unless you mean to do it deliberately. Like those bought penalties in my football career. You never knew where truth and falsehood crossed, where honesty and deception met and parted. And you could always blame the referee.

I never had much mail to deliver to Archina Kennedy. The occasional letter and now and again a parcel from a catalogue. She lived on her own and kept birds. Mostly canaries, but also budgies, and two parrots she called Bill and Ben. If you went near them, Bill cried out, 'Hallo, Ben,' and then Ben would call, 'Hallo, Bill,' and on and on they went greeting one another all day long until you left.

I had a parcel for her. Birdseed, most likely. She was at the well with her two buckets when I arrived.

'Can I give you a hand?'

'Only if you take both buckets,' she said. 'Otherwise, you'll be imbalanced and fall over.'

I gave her the parcel, put my post bag down by the well, and walked with her, a tin bucket in each hand, back to the house. She was right: the swing of one bucket balanced the other so that, strangely, I felt as if I was not carrying anything.

'Maybe I should do this with my post bag,' I said. 'Carry two. One off each shoulder so that it will feel like I'm carrying nothing.'

'It only works with water,' she said.

'Hullo, Bill,' Ben called as we passed, and Bill, of course, cried, 'Hullo, Ben.'

I put her buckets down next to the water-barrel Archina kept by the door.

'You'll take a plate of soup?' she said.

I knew not to refuse. It was lovely – a lentil broth

with her own home-made bread.

'You have something to show me?' she said, as soon as we finished our soup.

'I do?'

'Yes. A picture of lines and circles. I saw it in my sleep last night.'

I thought of denying it. This old woman's dreams.

'What kind of picture again?'

'Lines and circles and things.'

'I don't have it with me.'

'No. But you will next time you call by. Now, would you like some more soup? Or bread? No? I know, you've the postal run to do, and here I am holding you back. Take another slice of bread with you anyway. You can maybe feed the wild birds on the way. They get hungry too this time of the year.'

'Hallo, Bill, Hallo, Ben,' cried the parrots as I left.

'You know Archina?' I said to Charley when I got back from my round that night.

'Archina of the parrots?'

'Aye.'

'Says she had a dream last night. And asked me for the picture.'

'Of the writing?'

'Aye.'

'How…? You must have said something. Let slip something and she'd have heard.'

'Charley. No. I'm not that daft. No. I was delivering a parcel to her. Helped her with the water buckets from the well. She asked me in. Soup, and that wonderful bread she makes. And then in the midst of it all she suddenly said, "You have a picture to show me?" Of course I asked her what she meant and she said a picture with lines and circles on it and that she'd seen it in her sleep and wanted to see the image itself.'

'And what did you say? Did you say you would? Did you promise?'

'No. I didn't say anything. But Bill and Ben did. They said Hullo to one another again when I left.'

'And?'

'Well of course we should show it to her. Probably knows more already than all those professors. Will you come with me?'

'Well, I'm fishing till Saturday. Let's go then.'

Saturday was a misty drizzly smirry west coast of Scotland day. A tender day. One of those days when the drops of rain fall as dew, like a soft blessing on the earth. A small breeze keeps the midges away.

Archina was out digging with a spade in the garden when we arrived.

'The best time for cabbage,' she said.

She handed me the fork and Charley the hand hoe.

'Many hands make light work,' she said. 'Then we'll have the soup and bread.'

Once we finished, we washed our hands in the tub outside, with Bill and Ben still welcoming each other. Archina doled out three tureens of vegetable soup and her lovely bread and we sat there eating and blethering for a while.

'I brought the rubbing,' Charley said. She fetched it out of her haversack and handed it to Archina, who put it down on the table without looking at it.

'Do you know what it is already?' Charley asked.

Archina smiled.

'No. How would I? Nothing is ever certain. I too only see through a glass darkly.'

She picked up the image and looked at it for only a moment. She didn't speak.

'Does it say anything? Mean anything?'

'It says "tog seo agus bidh e na dhuslach anns an latha a bhios boinne uisge luach an òir". Which in English is "lift this and it will turn to dust in the day a drop of water is worth more than gold." That's what it says.'

'And means?'

'Let's go for the buckets of water.'

She stood and picked up the pails from the corner. Charley and I also took two pails each, and we walked down to the well, lowered our buckets into the water, and took them back to Archina's.

'Put two in the tub by the door,' she said. 'And two in the sink in the kitchen. And I'll put my two in the big kettles.'

'Maybe that's what it means,' she added. 'What's all the gold in the world worth if you haven't got your own well?'

She made a kettle of tea and asked us if we had any songs. Charley was a fine singer and sang 'Schubert's Nacht und Träume'. I sang 'Carrickfergus'. It was the only song I knew from start to finish, thanks to Pilfer who always sang in the pub after our Thames Caley matches:

> I wish I was in Carrickfergus
> Only for nights in Ballygrant
> I would swim over the deepest ocean
> The deepest ocean, my love to find
> But the sea is wide and I cannot swim over
> And neither have I wings to fly
> If I could find me a handsome boatman
> To ferry me over my love and I.

Archina then sang one of those long old Gaelic songs that sounded as if the sea itself was singing. As she sang, I thought, 'What if the sound of a song matters more than the meaning? *Is* the meaning? Maybe the search for the meaning of the words in the gold bar was itself the meaning?'

We gave Archina's translation to William Ross that evening.

'Meaningless twaddle,' he said. 'These parrots have driven her mad. Hallo, Bill. Hallo, Ben. Hallo, Bill. Hallo, Ben. Would drive anyone cuckoo. And anyway, what does it matter what the words say, except to scholars here and there, and obviously none of them can suss it out. You've already asked all those professors, haven't you, so you're as well listening to that old spey-wife. Her definition is as good as any. What matters is the actual value of the thing. Whether it's real gold. Proper gold. And if so, how much it's worth. And to do that we need to stop all this fucking about and take the bloody thing and get it weighed and measured and valued properly at a goldsmith's.'

It was quite the speech from William, who was usually more or less monosyllabic.

'Whatever,' we said. 'If that's what you want to do, William, do it.'

And he did. We didn't go with him to Rubh' na h-Achlais to collect the gold. Charley was away fishing, and I was doing my round, although if we'd really wanted to, we'd have accompanied him. We both feared seeing the thing literally crumbling to dust in his hands.

It didn't, for we saw him the next day.

'I'm taking it to London next week,' he said. 'See what value they put on it.'

It was valued at five to ten million pounds. Partially from the weight and volume of the gold itself, but mostly from the enormous historic value of the object. The gold dealer had checked with friends of his at the British Museum who said they'd never seen anything like it. That it was a unique historical artefact and should not be sold on the open market.

'We'd match any open market price for it,' the man at the museum said. 'As long as it hasn't been stolen or acquired illegally.'

William assured them it wasn't. It was a legitimately found object on public land, and even under the treasure trove law of Scotland, by which any such treasure belonged to the Crown, they would still have to pay the market value for it. So, we were – or at least William Ross was – sitting on a fortune. But Charley and I had no interest in either selling or gaining from it, whatever the fifty-fifty split or promise was or had been. He could keep it all for himself if he wanted. I think we decided that it wasn't ours to sell. Hadn't there been enough buying and selling? Offers and temptations and rewards. Chapman, who ended up in jail for abusing boys in his grasp. Who knows what might have happened had I accepted his bribe.

William Ross sold the ingot. I can't remember how much he eventually got for it, though I know he gave a substantial sum to the local community. I've no idea what he did with the rest of it, because he didn't run away to some sunny faraway island or buy an estate or a bigger house or anything. He kept his stone-masoning business going on as before, building walls here and renovating houses there.

'You never know what things I might discover in these ruins,' he'd say when I met him.

The gold stone itself lies behind protected glass in the British Museum. Scholars remove and inspect it now and again, still trying to decipher, digitally these days, what the writing means. They believe Archina made her translation up, though Archina told us that the meaning had been given to her in a dream by Olghair MacCoinnich himself.

'They will refuse to believe until the very day it crumbles in their hands,' she said.

14

NO ONE ON The Island said much. Now and again, someone might say, 'William Ross is doing well, eh?'

Or one of the care workers would say how thankful she was for his donation to the care home. 'We managed to get a wee bus, and it's so lovely, because we can take the residents out for a run. It's so nice for them to see and remember places they'd forgotten about.'

But for most folk the story about the finding of the secret gold tablet faded into the background, like most other news.

'Did you hear the latest about Councillor Fraser?'

'What? What was that you said? No! I don't believe it.'

'The thing is, ducks are much easier to keep than hens. They can fend for themselves so much better. I tell you! It's true.'

'China? I told you it would lead to a world war.'

'I'm not sure he ever found that gold thing over at that Rubh' na h-Achlais. Who in his right mind would ever leave such a thing there, in a cave, down the side of a cliff?'

'Pirates? Pirates, maybe, on the run after the Armada?'

After the news had quietened down, I saw Archina again, as ever, working her fields and garden. Lifting the potatoes from her patch high above the stream. I walked up with my bag and gave her a letter, and she signalled for me to stay. She sat down on a tuft of grass on top of the hillock and I sat down opposite. I had my lunch bite in my haversack, and she had her own bread and cheese wrapped in a cloth in the small wicker basket she sometimes carried on her back. She went down the hill and filled her jug with water from the flowing stream. She always poured the first jug back into the stream before filling it again.

'The first drink to the host,' she said.

We ate in silence, as if it was a holy thing. We could hear the stream. And the birds chirping away. Some silent butterflies weaved in and out amongst the leaves of the potato stalks. I wondered whether they'd alight on the nightshade flowers, but they floated past, down towards the primroses and violets and orchids growing by the stream's edge.

'These dreams of yours?' I asked her. 'They're just memories and hopes and imaginings and things, all strung together to cast a future, aren't they?'

She laughed.

'Dear boy, you could say that about everything, could you not?'

'I suppose so.'

She was looking down towards the water.

'You could say that about the stream. And the

orchids and primroses and violets and those butterflies we watched winging their way down there. Do you think, for a moment, that they don't mean anything? That they're not telling you something?'

But that's different, I wanted to say. I didn't. That's so different from telling me you dreamt you saw the writing from the gold. And that Olghair MacKenzie, dead for centuries, then told you what it meant?

And suddenly she startled me.

'Remember Sally? She was my granddaughter. Her dad, who was killed in a motorcycle accident, was my son. My dear, darling Robbie. And because he was born before I was married, I was never given the honour of being Sally's granny. Though she used to come here secretly and we shared so many things. She loved you. But you know that. And I know that, in the same way as I know what Olghair MacKenzie thought and said and did. He was her great-grandfather, seven times over. So you see, Jack, everything knits together, and you're part of that dream, as you call it. As are the butterflies down there, and the orchids and the primroses and the violets and the stream. Without them, too, the dream cannot be told.'

I thought about football. Goalie, right back, left back, midfield, striker. The periodic table. Hydrogen, lithium, sodium. The gorgeous patterns my mum created in the Fair Isle jerseys she knitted – The Indian Acre and The Daisy and The Crested Wave and The Three Waves – or the ugly ones in the weather as another gale force wind swept in from the west, threatening her carefully planted flowers. Shannon Rockhall Malin Hebrides, wind variable 2 to 4, becoming southeast then cyclonic 5 to 7, occasionally gale 8 later, Sea State, moderate becoming rough, weather, showers then rain, visibility, good becoming moderate or poor.

The patterns we're trained to see, where one element links to another, so that you see a design, or a world, that's all connected and dependent, instead of loose ends and things lying about here and there as in old Johnny's house, where you were as likely to sit on a duck as on a cushion, and pick up a cat instead of a book when you put your hand on a shelf. The rhythms of song and poetry trying to make sense of it all. I must go down to the seas again, to the lonely sea and the sky, and all I ask for is a tall ship and a star to steer her by. Those Gaelic songs that rise and fall like the tide, and the tides which come and go so that Charley can work out where to cast her creels to catch the best lobsters. And the arched bridge in the shape of a perfect wave, sloshing us backwards and forwards, to and fro, from here to there, as in a cradle.

Archina is now long gone. As are Mary MacLaren and Nosey Shaw and Elsie MacInnes and Mrs Hall, with all their knowledge. Their language. Their loneliness.

Despite all the new houses and new residents and wider roads and faster traffic, what remains is the scent. As you come over the bridge, the smell of wild garlic and buddleia and lilac swirls through the open car window, as it always did.

Charley and I have worked wonders in the garden

that was once Johnny's. The major part is given over to a herb and flower garden which we've filled, over the years, with seeds and bulbs and flowers, colours and fragrances that have become almost obsolete. Little old-fashioned things (including garden gnomes!) we've gathered from collectors here and there, and though some of them haven't survived the west coast salty air and wind and gales and rain, we continue to be surprised how resilient the natural things in the world are: bluebells and primroses and thistles and nettles (which make the finest of soups!).

Every time we cross the bridge we think of Olghair MacKenzie. I doubt he liked flowers and herbs and perfumes, but who knows, for the evidence we leave is only partial, and always left to others as a kind of puzzle. Now if only he had created an ingot made of buddleia and lilac instead of gold, I doubt William Ross would have had any interest.

But then again, maybe that's exactly what he did leave, forging his future into a prophecy that only Archina Henderson Kennedy could decipher. Last week, Charley and I were about to have lunch and switched on the One O' Clock News. One of the stories was the Prime Minister's visit to the British Museum. He was so taken with what they labelled 'MacKenzie's Gold Ingot' that he asked special permission to hold it. When it was placed into his hands it instantly crumbled into dust, sending thousands of gold flakes spiralling into the air like confetti before falling as hard rain.

15

AFTER MUM DIED, I had to deal with the house and its contents. The house went on the market and all the furniture was either given to local charities or opened to valuation by the local auctioneer.

First I went through things so that no personal items – letters and family photographs and so on – would be lost. Dad's writing desk was as it had been the day he died. It was one of those old-fashioned desks with twelve small drawers, a selection of pigeon-holes across the top, and four deeper drawers on each side. Only the bottom drawer was locked, and once I got Smith, the local joiner, to prize it open, all Dad's papers were inside. Drawings and charts and maps and a long hand-written history of Olghair MacKenzie. Born in Perth in 1556, educated at the Grammar School before going on to study Divinity, Logic, Philosophy, and Law at St Andrew's University and then moving abroad.

The information was more or less as Archina MacLaren had told me, except with more detail. In 1576 going to the Scots College in Paris then to the University of Salamanca where he studied under Francisco de Vitoria and on to Rome to study Canon Law, then across to Salonika and Constantinople before settling in Safed where he got involved with a congregation of Sephardic Jews newly returned to the Ottoman Empire from their exile in Spain. They initiated Olghair MacKenzie into the ways of mysticism, specifically the kabbalistic doctrine and extreme asceticism. After some years there he moved south, first to Alexandria and then to Cairo. Influenced by teaching from Persia, India, and Byzantium, he became convinced that everything he had learned could be gathered into one comprehensive system, meaning you couldn't heal the body without healing the spirit first, and you couldn't heal the mind without healing the body too. 'To give a cup of water to a thirsty man,' he wrote, 'is to heal him of all pain, past, present and future. The word must become flesh.'

Dad's writing was of a kind I'd never seen before. Of course I knew his writing – I'd seen it so often as he stood with his chalk at the blackboard writing out sentences or equations. $345 \times 5 = 1725$. The quick brown fox jumps over the lazy dog. Sometimes we all got a shot at writing it out in chalk on the board. Sally always used big spidery letters.

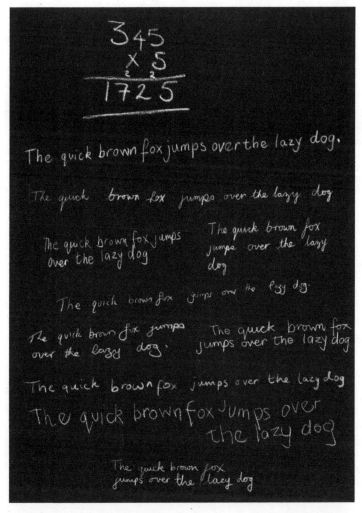

And of course I also knew his writing intimately from the private letters he wrote to me when I first went down to Chelsea, with that assured slanted dark blue fountain pen he treasured:

Dear Jack,

I trust everything is going well for you in London. Mum and I are well and keeping ourselves busy as usual. The garden, thanks to Mum's efforts, is looking glorious in the late Spring sunshine, and I am busy marking things up for the Summer Term! I am so looking forward to that time, with the long clear nights when it hardly gets dark at all.

As you know, these are my favourite times for walking across the moors and camping out overnight. I have made some fascinating discoveries over among the cliffs on the western shore and maybe, after all, now that you're grown up, you can come along with me sometime to see these things yourself. Everything's secret until it's discovered, or put there. You could be Ben Gunn and I can be Long John Silver!

There is much to be done, but I am willing to believe I can do it. For if we don't do it, somebody else will do it instead and get it all wrong. But you will probably be too busy, and I know you will have

training and a Summer tour to do where you are, so it might have to wait for later on.

We miss you, but I hope to mannge down to see you before too long and I look forward to getting all your news then.
Dad (and Mum, currently outside weeding the earlies!)

He wrote capital letters, the Ds and Ms and Ss and Ts, with certainty and a bit of a flourish. But he wrote the letter 'e', with those three hands, as if he couldn't quite make up his mind whether it was a small e or a capital E. So the written history of Olghair MacKenzie was not some ancient document, but something Dad had written. Or perhaps copied from some ancient scroll. Maybe it didn't matter. Maybe it was the simple magic of time, transforming things before our very eyes.

And there, beneath the written story, I saw the map of the family tree, tracing us back through five centuries to Olghair MacCoinnich, born in Perth, Scotland in 1556 to Father Unknown and Mairianna MacKenzie of River Lodge, Scone. And how could I have been so innocent? Olghair, the original Gaelic (or at least Germanic) name for Oliver. My father's middle name: Alasdair Oliver MacKenzie. As it was my own, though neither he nor I ever used it. Jack Oliver MacKenzie. He had made himself the hero of the story: which is, after all, the only way to live.

He was Olghair. As I was. And as I studied the written history and the family tree and the sketches and drawings and compass and map markings and brushes and glue and flakes of gold my father left in the drawer, I knew that's what his Friday evening camping expeditions and Saturday walks had been all about: building a rickety bridge between here and there, always shining gold under the eighth moon, folk forever walking across, carrying their football boots and skates and lobster creels and flowers and stones and cups of tea and all kinds of odds and ends, becoming treasures on the way.

Jack Olghair MacCoinnich, witness confirmatio.

Acknowledgements

Thanks to Gavin MacDougall, Amy Turnbull, Jennie Renton and the team at Luath Press for their help in making and distributing this book. To Francoise Marché-Latour for her advice on French, and for proof-reading. A special thanks to Gwyneth Findlay who edited the book with care and encouragement, and to Liondsaidh Chaimbeul for the illustrations. Tapadh leibh uile.

Some other books published by **LUATH PRESS**

Electricity
Angus Peter Campbell
ISBN 9781804250501 PBK £9.99

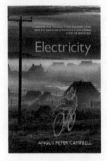

Shortlisted for the Saltire Scottish Fiction Book of the Year 2023

Taking a step back into her Hebridean childhood, Granny writes to her granddaughter in Australia, decorating her notebooks with hand-drawn scribbles and doodles. Though she may now live in Edinburgh, she relives her memories with a sense of warmth and protection.

I enjoyed this book immensely. It reads beautifully, a novel which is as much an act of reverence as a work of fiction.—LOUIS DE BERNIÈRES

An enchanting novel and a kind one … the sentiment here rings diamond-true.—ALLAN MASSIE, THE SCOTSMAN

A joy from beginning to end.
—KAREN MATHESON

Memory and Straw
Angus Peter Campbell
ISBN 9781912147410 PBK £7.99

Winner of the Saltire Scottish Fiction Book of the Year 2017

Gavin and Emma live in Manhattan. She's a musician. He works in Artificial Intelligence. He's good at his job. Scarily good. He's researching human features to make more realistic mask-bots – non-human 'carers' for elderly people. When his enquiry turns personal he's forced to ask whether his own life is an artificial mask.

A glorious adventure in voices, it sifts through memory and randomness, what we retain and do not, the vividness of the fragments that inexplicably linger in technicolour, and our own, never-outgrown, absurdity… An irrepressible, quite remarkable, joy.
—JANICE GALLOWAY

The Girl on the Ferryboat

Angus Peter Campbell
ISBN 9781910021187 PBK £7.99

It was a long hot summer...
a chance encounter on a ferry
leads to a lifetime of regret for
misplaced opportunities.

Beautifully written and
vividly evoked, *The Girl on
the Ferryboat* is a mirage
of recollections looking
back to the haze of one final
prelapsarian summer on the
Isle of Mull.

*Campbell's writing [is]
transcendently beautiful...
a delight in any language.*
—SCOTLAND ON SUNDAY

*Unlikely but memorable love
story.*—DAILY MAIL

*A touching human story which
really is wonderfully written.*
—SCOTTISH FIELD

Archie and the North Wind

Angus Peter Campbell
ISBN 9781906817381 PBK £8.99

Archie genuinely believes
the old legends he was told
as a child. Growing up on a
small island off the Scottish
coast and sheltered from the
rest of the world, despite
all the knowledge he gains
as an adult, he still believes
in the underlying truth of
these stories. After years of
unemployment, to escape his
selfish wife and to stop the
North Wind from blowing so
harshly in winter, Archie leaves
home to find the hole where the
North Wind originates. Funny,
original and very moving,
Archie and the North Wind
demonstrates the raw power of
storytelling.

A vitally important writer...
—NEW STATESMAN

Details of these and other books published by Luath Press can be found at:
www.luath.co.uk

Luath Press Limited

committed to publishing well written books worth reading

LUATH PRESS takes its name from Robert Burns, whose little collie Luath (*Gael.*, swift or nimble) tripped up Jean Armour at a wedding and gave him the chance to speak to the woman who was to be his wife and the abiding love of his life. Burns called one of the 'Twa Dogs' Luath after Cuchullin's hunting dog in Ossian's *Fingal*. Luath Press was established in 1981 in the heart of Burns country, and is now based a few steps up the road from Burns' first lodgings on Edinburgh's Royal Mile. Luath offers you distinctive writing with a hint of unexpected pleasures.

Most bookshops in the UK, the US, Canada, Australia, New Zealand and parts of Europe, either carry our books in stock or can order them for you. To order direct from us, please send a £sterling cheque, postal order, international money order or your credit card details (number, address of cardholder and expiry date) to us at the address below. Please add post and packing as follows: UK – £1.00 per delivery address; overseas surface mail – £2.50 per delivery address; overseas airmail – £3.50 for the first book to each delivery address, plus £1.00 for each additional book by airmail to the same address. If your order is a gift, we will happily enclose your card or message at no extra charge.

Luath Press Limited
543/2 Castlehill
The Royal Mile
Edinburgh EH1 2ND
Scotland
Telephone: 0131 225 4326 (24 hours)
Email: sales@luath.co.uk
Website: www.luath.co.uk